Why am I doing this? *Wren wondered to herself.* **He's nothing to me but trouble.**

Because Keegan was in need. Because it was two days before Christmas and because on some subterranean level, she related to this man. And because, if Wren dared to admit it, she was wildly attracted to him with an intensity that shocked and surprised her.

Who was Mr. Keegan Winslow? Everything about him was contradictory, from his secretive demeanor to the fact that he'd milked her cows the night before. Wren, with her limited experience where the opposite sex was concerned, hardly knew what to make of this masculine creature who had come to roost in her loft.

Yet something told her that deep inside, Keegan Winslow was an honest and decent man who'd fallen on hard times. Nevertheless, she wasn't about to let herself entertain any sort of romantic notions about him.

What was wrong with her for even considering such thoughts?

Dear Reader,

Happy Holidays! Our gift to you is all the very best Romance has to offer, starting with *A Kiss, a Kid and a Mistletoe Bride* by RITA-Award winning author Lindsay Longford. In this VIRGIN BRIDES title, when a single dad returns home at Christmas, he encounters the golden girl he'd fallen for one magical night a lifetime ago. Can his kiss—and his kid—win her heart and make her a mistletoe mom?

Rising star Susan Meier continues her TEXAS FAMILY TIES miniseries with *Guess What? We're Married!* And no one is more shocked than the amnesiac bride in this sexy, surprising story! In *The Rich Gal's Rented Groom,* the next sparkling installment of Carolyn Zane's THE BRUBAKER BRIDES, a rugged ranch hand poses as Patsy Brubaker's husband at her ten-year high school reunion. But this gal voted Most Likely To Succeed won't rest till she wins her counterfeit hubby's heart! BUNDLES OF JOY meets BACHELOR GULCH in a fairy-tale romance by beloved author Sandra Steffen. When a shy beauty is about to accept *another* man's proposal, her true-blue *true* love returns to town, bearing *Burke's Christmas Surprise.*

Who wouldn't want to be *Stranded with a Tall, Dark Stranger*— especially an embittered ex-cop in need of a good woman's love? Laura Anthony's tale of transformation is perfect for the holidays! And speaking of transformations… Hayley Gardner weaves an adorable, uplifting tale of a Grinch-like hero who becomes a Santa Claus daddy when he receives *A Baby in His Stocking.*

And in the New Year, look for our fabulous new promotion FAMILY MATTERS and Romance's first-ever six-book continuity series, LOVING THE BOSS, in which office romance leads six friends down the aisle.

Happy Holidays!

Mary-Theresa Hussey
Senior Editor, Silhouette Romance

Please address questions and book requests to:
Silhouette Reader Service
U.S.: 3010 Walden Ave., P.O. Box 1325, Buffalo, NY 14269
Canadian: P.O. Box 609, Fort Erie, Ont. L2A 5X3

STRANDED WITH A TALL, DARK STRANGER

Laura Anthony

Silhouette

R O M A N C E™

Published by Silhouette Books

America's Publisher of Contemporary Romance

To Hebby—
For all those long, late-night telephone conversations.
You're a great friend. Thanks for standing by me
when things got tough. You'll never know how much
your friendship means to me.

SILHOUETTE BOOKS

ISBN 0-373-19340-8

STRANDED WITH A TALL, DARK STRANGER

Copyright © 1998 by Laurie Blalock

Printed in U.S.A.

Books by Laura Anthony

Silhouette Romance

Raleigh and the Rancher #1092
Second Chance Family #1119
Undercover Honeymoon #1166
Look-Alike Bride #1220
Baby Business #1240
The Stranger's Surprise #1260
Bride of a Texas Trueblood #1285
Honey of a Husband #1322
Stranded with a Tall, Dark Stranger #1340

LAURA ANTHONY

started writing at age eight. She credits her father, Fred Blalock, as the guiding force behind her career. Although a registered nurse, Laura has achieved a life-long dream and now pursues writing fiction full-time. Her hobbies include jogging, boating, traveling and reading voraciously.

Chapter One

Wren Matthews took the last of the cranberry-walnut bread from her oven and set the small loaves to cool on the oak sideboard. The aromas of fresh baked bread and hot coffee mingled with the hearty scent of beef stew simmering on the back burner.

Jaunty strains of Brenda Lee's "Rocking around the Christmas Tree," issued from the transistor radio perched on the windowsill, blunting the sound of the winter weather howling outside her door. Yesterday, it had been a sunny seventy degrees. This morning however, the temperature had plummeted, bringing with it a vibrant electrical storm.

She had finished her Christmas baking just in time to start the evening milking. At the thought of the heavy chores waiting for her, Wren sighed and closed the oven door.

Sometimes the overwhelming responsibility had her thinking of selling the dairy and moving into town, but she simply couldn't bring herself to part with the farm.

The modest homestead had been in the Matthews family for three generations. She simply couldn't dishonor her parents' memory by giving up.

Wren washed her hands at the sink and peered out at the gangly cottonwood limbs whipping in the wind. The branches made an eerie scratching noise against the screen.

It was tough running the place on her own. If only she could find reliable help. Someone to live in the loft apartment over the barn. Someone strong and hardworking. Someone who would keep to himself and leave her alone.

Perhaps she should advertise for a dairy hand in the local paper. For a while one of the boys from the high school, where she taught freshman English, had assisted her. Then six weeks ago Jeff had injured his knee playing football and Wren found herself struggling to meet the dual obligations of school-teaching and dairy farming. Thank heavens for Christmas break. With any luck, she would find someone before school resumed session in the new year.

Problem was, strangers terrified her. She was shy around people she didn't know. Very shy. She required a boarder as introverted as herself. Someone who wouldn't want to talk her ear off or become fast friends. Someone who preferred solitude as much as she did.

Turning off the oven, she untied her flour-stained, red-and-green apron, with miniature Santa Clauses embroidered across the front, and draped it over the cabinet. She limped to the back door. Her old hip injury flared in damp weather and, much as she hated to succumb to the pain, she'd been forced to down two aspirins earlier that evening.

"And now it's time for the six o'clock news," the disk jockey purred, followed by lead-in music.

Half listening to the broadcast, Wren worked her feet into the yellow rubber boots she'd left drying on newspaper spread over the parquet entryway.

While the radio announcer gave a rundown on world and state news, Wren went about her business. Lifting her heavy down jacket from the brass coat tree in the corner, she then shrugged into the garment and pulled on worn leather gloves extracted from one pocket.

"The storm moving through Texas is expected to worsen late tonight, plunging temperatures to an all-time record low," the announcer warned. "Bring the pets and plants inside and don't drive if at all possible."

A chill chased down Wren's spine at the cold winter weather wailing like a mournful banshee around the wooden door frame. If it weren't for the cattle, she'd make sure the door was locked tight, crawl inside her four-poster bed with a cup of hot chocolate and watch a rerun of *It's a Wonderful Life* and forget all about that dreary forecast.

But she didn't have that luxury. The cows had to be milked and she was the only one to do it.

Here goes, she thought and rested her hand on the knob at the same time a knock barked at the door.

The sudden noise reverberated in the room like a gunshot blast.

Startled, Wren jumped and jerked back her hand. Her stomach churned and trepidation rose in her chest.

Pressing a palm to her mouth, she waited, praying that she'd imagined the commotion. Perhaps it had been a tree branch breaking loose from its moorings and slamming against the side of the house.

She waited.

The knock came again, denying any fanciful explanations she'd been concocting.

Who could be visiting in this storm? she wondered. Trepidation dissolved into apprehension. Any deviation from the norm was immediate cause for concern.

She didn't get many guests out this far from town— her pastor, some of the little old ladies from her church, one or two teachers from the high school, that was about it. In Stephenville, she was known as the kooky crippled spinster who lived all alone on her aging dairy farm and who, at the naive age of nineteen, had once been swindled by a charming con man. Even now, ten years later, Wren blushed at the memory of Blaine Thomas and her youthful mistake.

She'd been lonely and vulnerable after her parents' death. Easy pickings for the likes of smooth, butter-wouldn't-melt-in-his-mouth Blaine Thomas. He'd used flattery and compliments to make her feel loved when he'd only been after her money. She'd almost lost the farm because of her foolishness and she'd sworn never again to trust a man. Particularly a handsome one.

The knock was bolder, more insistent this time.

Who could it be? Standing there with her head cocked, she struggled to muster enough courage to move forward and investigate.

Maybe it's a neighbor in distress, she scolded herself. *You can't leave someone standing out in the rain.*

And yet the snake of fear winding around her heart kept her rooted firmly to the floor. Wren placed her hands over her ears. *Go away, go away, go away,* she silently chanted.

"Is anyone home?"

The voice was strong, masculine, demanding, and

served to escalate Wren's dread and sharpen her sense
of isolation.

"I need help."

Too readily, she recalled those terrifying moments
eleven years ago. In the wee hours of the morning she
had found herself in a similar situation, dragging her
wounded body from door to door, begging people to let
her in while her parents' mangled car lay overturned on
an icy street. She had practically crawled on her crumpled, bleeding leg and she'd gone to three houses before
a kindly middle-aged couple had finally opened their
door to her.

"Please?"

That single word rent her heart and snuck past her
defenses as nothing else would have. What if this man
needed her as badly as she'd needed assistance that awful night her parents died?

Resolutely, she put the chain on the door then edged
it open a tiny crack. A streak of lightning illuminated
the ebony sky, highlighting the figure on her porch.

A hulking stranger loomed in the darkness. The sight
of him snatched air from her lungs. Gasping, Wren
slapped a hand over her mouth and took a step backward.

The man was very tall, towering many inches above
her own petite five-foot-two-inch frame, and he was
powerfully built, with wide shoulders and large muscular
arms. He wore a battered fedora that reminded her of
Indiana Jones and a black leather jacket that conjured an
even more dangerous image.

His dark eyes were deep-set and watchful, his countenance enigmatic and forbidding. A chill ran through
Wren at his assessment.

"I'm stranded," he said.

His sharp, clipped speech told her the man wasn't a Texan. A Northerner, she surmised. Chicago, perhaps?

He waited expectantly, his head angled to one side, rain blowing into the house around him. Instinct begged her to slam the door and lock it tight against him and yet she hesitated.

"What do you want?" Wren squeaked, her heart pounding, one hand wrapped protectively around the door.

"To come in from the wet and cold."

He spoke in a commanding timbre. His voice reminded Wren of the eerie tone her father had used when he had told ghost stories around the campfire.

"I'm sorry," she shook her head. "I can't help you." She began easing the door closed.

"I understand," he said. "I don't blame you. I wouldn't take a stranger into my home either." Hunching his shoulders, he turned and started down the steps.

Wren slammed the door behind him, and slid the dead bolt home. Her pulse, thready and weak, slipped through her veins like water. Her whole body trembled violently and she had to sag against the door to keep from falling.

Maybe she should call someone. Tell them she was alone with a stranger at the door. But who could she call?

Taking a deep breath, she tried to calm down. "Steady, Wren, just step across the floor to the phone and notify the sheriff. That's all you've got to do," she spoke out loud.

That was easier said than done. Ugly images kept springing into her mind. Images of that dark, threatening stranger standing outside her window with a sharp knife clutched in his hand, waiting for the opportunity to hurt her.

"Stop it," she hissed under her breath. "Call the sheriff. Now."

Wren put one foot in front of the other, clenching her jaw to block out any other unnecessary visions. Her fingers shook and she dropped the receiver twice before she managed to get it to her ear.

Sterile silence.

The line was dead.

The stranger slogged through the driving sleet, disappointed but not surprised. Over the course of the last six months, he'd grown accustomed to such treatment. He expected it. But he wasn't opposed to trespassing, especially since the lady's barn appeared so inviting.

A light shone through the barn window and he could hear cattle lowing restlessly from behind closed doors. It was a dairy farm, he rationalized, the barn was bound to be heated and he'd slept in worse places. If nothing else, he'd have milk to drink and a dry place to rest his head.

He'd frightened the woman pretty badly. She reminded him of a timid mouse, all wide-eyed and twitchy. She was one of the those quiet women men rarely noticed. Not unattractive, but definitely nothing that snagged one's interest. She lived alone, he surmised and he doubted that she was brave enough to come into the barn looking for him. This would be as good a place as any to hole up for the night. He'd be gone by morning and she never need know he'd lingered here.

With a backward glance over his shoulder at the house, the stranger turned and entered the large barn.

The cows greeted him loud and hearty, clearly expecting to be milked. The stranger closed the door behind him and shook off the wet cold. The warm air offered a welcome respite and for the first time in many hours he felt free to relax his guard.

His gaze fell on a stairwell leading to an overhead loft. Raising a curious eyebrow, he went to investigate, moving past over a dozen stalls of well-fed Holsteins.

He climbed the stairs and pushed open the door into the small sparse room. A cot covered with a worn woolen army blanket sat in one corner, an unplugged space heater rested beside it. There was a sink on the opposite side wall and a toilet cloaked behind a flowered shower curtain. Primitive but functional.

A smile curled his wind-blistered lips. Perfect.

"Okay, just because the phone is dead doesn't mean he cut the line," Wren said, trying desperately to hearten herself. "It's probably the storm. Remember, the phones went out twice last winter."

Her pathetic reassurances did nothing to comfort her internal quaking. Was the man still prowling out there in the night?

Terrified at the thought, Wren went to every window, and made sure they were securely locked and the curtains drawn. She darted occasional glances into the darkness beyond, knowing that if she looked out to see a face staring back at her, she'd have a heart attack and die on the spot.

From the kitchen, her transistor radio inanely played on, heedless of her situation. "I Saw Mommy Kissing Santa Claus" flowed into "Grandma Got Run Over By a Reindeer." The rollicking, tongue-in-cheek ditty provided a direct contrast to the turmoil generated by the stranger's mysterious arrival. She thought about turning the radio off but the prospect of eerie silence was even more unsettling than the merry music.

She folded her hands together and began to pace, favoring her aching hip. She wondered what to do next. Even through the storm and the song, Wren could hear the cows calling. She glanced at the clock on the wall, saw it was well after six-thirty. The ruckus from the barn would only get louder as the cows grew more distended with milk.

"I can't go out there," she muttered.

Wren quivered at the prospect. The thought of treading out into the freezing rain with the interloper on the loose had Wren biting the inside of her cheek.

Perhaps he's gone.

And perhaps he's not.

Distressed, she plopped down at the kitchen table and drummed her fingers over the scarred oak. What to do? A bellowing noise, louder and more insistent than a foghorn, mingled with the shrieking wind and created a nerve-racking cacophony. There was no mistaking Bossie's distinctive clamor. She was the oldest cow in Wren's seventeen-head herd and quite spoiled.

"You can't hide in here all night, Wren," she chided herself. "The cows have to be milked."

But it can wait, her cautious side argued. *Give that dark stranger time to mosey on down the road.*

Her sense of responsibility warred with her natural timidity. Finally, Wren struck a bargain with herself. She'd eat supper first, then go milk the cows.

Scraping back her chair on the worn floor, she shrugged out of her coat before going over to the stove. She dished up stew in a bowl and retrieved a handful of saltines from the cracker jar. Taking her time, she poured herself a cup of hot tea before settling back in at the table with her meal.

The racket from the barn increased, rising in both

tempo and intensity. She blew on a spoonful of stew to cool it and tried her best to tune out the cows' miserable cries, but the food stuck in her throat. Swallowing down the bite, she sat staring at her soup bowl.

She couldn't eat. Not now. Not when she was so upset, not with the cows begging to be milked.

"And now, Sloan Clayton, with the seven o'clock news." The radio crackled as lightning jumped outside the window.

Thunder grumbled and Wren tightened her grip on the spoon handle, the assault of sounds almost too much to bear.

"Worsening weather is the hour's top story," the news announcer said. "Driving rain is rapidly turning to sleet and the temperature has already dropped ten degrees in less than an hour, with an expected low in the single digits."

As if in recognition of his proclamation, Wren shivered. There was no way she could continue to ignore the cattle. She had to make sure they were warm enough, that the heaters were still working.

"The National Weather Service has issued a severe winter weather advisory. Motorists are cautioned to stay off the roads if at all possible."

Idly, Wren crushed a cracker with the palm of her hand. She couldn't help thinking about that man, out there alone in the wet and cold. Sighing, she pushed her soup bowl across the table. Why she should suddenly feel sorry for the stranger mystified her.

Inclining her head, she dusted the cracker crumbs from her hands. Suddenly, the decreased noise level caught her attention.

The cows had stopped mooing.

Wren froze in her seat. Why?

Her stomach tingled as if she'd eaten a thousand hot chili peppers and her mouth was very dry. Wren got up and turned down the radio. She waited in the middle of the kitchen, head cocked, pulse racing.

Nothing but the wind howling through the trees.

She bit her bottom lip in consternation. The cows should be getting louder, not shutting up entirely. This was too weird.

Go investigate, her conscience prodded.

But Wren stayed rooted to the spot. *I'm scared.*

Coward.

She wadded her hands into fists. She couldn't stay here all night, cowering in fear. She had to find out what was going on in the barn, no matter how frightening the prospect.

Heaving in a deep breath to bolster her courage, Wren donned her coat and gloves once more, took a tiny gold key from a rack over the sink and went to the living room to unlock her father's gun cabinet.

She peered at the array of firearms. She knew next to nothing about guns and had only used the .22 on occasion to kill rattlesnakes and copperheads. Wren wrapped a gloved hand around the wooden stock and lifted the weapon from its home. Carefully, she locked the cabinet and dropped the key into her pocket.

Could she use the gun on a human being? Wren gulped.

"You can do whatever you have to do to survive," she said, "now, come on."

Armed with the lightweight .22-caliber semiautomatic, she switched off the safety and headed out the door. Clinging to the barrel, with her finger poised near the trigger, Wren struggled through the wind, her hip aching in response to the sorry weather.

She darted furtive looks left and right but, save for the light from the barn, she saw nothing but pitch blackness. A man could be skulking behind any tree, beside any fence, around any corner.

Fear rose high and heavy inside her belly. She clutched the gun tighter. Sleet pelted down on her rain cap and slapped her face with startling cold. She kept her head down, her chin tucked to her chest.

Lightning slashed the dark sky. Thunder rumbled like artillery fire. The air smelled harsh, metallic, with the odor of electricity.

Wren couldn't see more than a few feet in front of her and her teeth chattered in response to the biting cold. Thick mud clung to her boots, throwing her off balance. She stumbled and trudged forward, fighting the ooze and her escalating terror.

It was a relief to burst into the barn at last, even though she didn't know what she might find hiding there. She kept the gun raised and her back to the wall.

Wren blinked against the brightness, her breath coming in reedy wheezes. What she saw sent her blood pumping swiftly through her ear drums.

The cattle were placidly munching oats at their troughs, happily hooked to the milking machines.

What was going on?

Feeling as if she'd stepped into the Twilight Zone, Wren battled the surreal sensation, cleared her throat and tried to speak but it seemed the words were trapped in her voice box, unable to get out.

Frantically, she scanned the barn and saw nothing amiss.

The man had to be in here. Who else could have done this?

Sweat flooded her brow and Wren gripped the rifle

with all her strength. Why would he hook her cows to the milking machines? Did he have some ulterior motive or had he simply grown deaf listening to them bellow?

It didn't matter. She'd started down this road and now she had to finish her journey. Gun butt resting against her shoulder, she squinted down the .22's sight, as she aimed the weapon and stepped carefully past each stall.

One, two, three. Her heart revved faster with each advancing step. Bossie switched her tail and leveled a sassy look at Wren.

Four, five, six.

Empty. Empty. Empty.

Seven, eight, nine, ten. The smell of oats lay strong. Hay rustled beneath her boots.

Eleven, twelve, thirteen.

No one.

Fourteen, fifteen, sixteen, seventeen.

All cows accounted for and no stranger in view.

The hairs on the back of Wren's neck stood at full attention. She rounded the refrigerated milking vat and peeked into every nook and cranny, the nose of the gun preceding her every move.

Nothing.

Slowly, she swung her eyes upward, knowing without a doubt the stranger was in the loft.

Probably watching her through a knothole.

Did he have a gun? That thought deepened her fear. What was she going to do? If she ran back to the house, she wouldn't be able to call the police and she'd be trapped once more, effectively giving the stranger the upper hand. At least this way she possessed the advantage.

So what now? Climb the stairs? Hang back? Wait?

One course of action remained. Confront him.

Her knees weak with the prospect, Wren swayed on her feet. "Okay, mister, I know you're up there," she said, surprised by how authoritative her voice sounded. "I've got a gun trained on the stairs. You better come on down before I start shooting first and asking questions later."

Chapter Two

The stranger hesitated, poised at the loft door. Through a slit in the rough-hewn boards, he could see the woman moving around below, a puny .22-caliber rifle clutched in her trembling arms. He cocked one eyebrow in surprise. He'd underestimated her grit. He'd pegged her as being far too timid for such a bold maneuver.

She was nervous and scared but she'd been brave enough to venture out to the barn in this weather, knowing full well he was probably ensconced inside. His estimation of her climbed a notch.

It had been a mistake to hook the cows up to the milking machines, he surmised, but the infernal bellowing had been too much to tolerate. Undoubtedly, the sudden silence had lured the woman into the barn to investigate.

"Mister, I'm not kidding."

Her voice rose slightly. If he hadn't been trained to recognize such nuances he might not have noticed, but the increase in her anxiety level warned him she might indeed shoot first and ask questions later. He might as well go introduce himself before he ended up with a bullet in his butt.

Sighing, he lifted his hands over his head in the universal signal of surrender. "Please, don't shoot." He stopped halfway down the steps.

She had the barrel aimed square at his belly. "What are you doing here?" she demanded. "I told you to leave my property."

"Listen," he began, "I apologize for trespassing but it's too damned cold to spend the night outdoors."

"Climb to the floor," she said, trying her best to screw her mouth into a deadly scowl. Instead, she looked rather comical—like a little girl playing cop.

He obeyed, not because he was frightened of her threats but because he suspected she wasn't well versed in the use of firearms. "I'm not going to hurt you," he said. "I just wanted a place out of the weather."

"Did you hook my cows to the milking machine?" She jutted her small chin firmly forward.

"Yes."

"Why?"

"I was tired of listening to the noise."

"Where did you learn to run a milking machine?" she demanded.

"My grandfather owned a dairy in upstate Wisconsin. I spent a few summers there as a kid."

"So you just took it upon yourself to milk my cows." Ire flashed in her eyes. Spunky. He liked that.

"I did. You got a problem?"

She frowned. "I got a problem with your attitude, mister. Remember, I'm the one with the gun."

If he hadn't been so tired, the stranger would have been tempted to smile at her naiveté. "Lady, there's a

.357 Magnum resting across my shoulders, if I were interested in harming you, I could have shot you the minute you stepped through the door.''

Her face blanched as she considered what he was telling her. "Then you better throw your gun down."

He sighed. "I don't really want to do that."

Taking a step forward, she placed the rifle's nose flush against his belly button. "Throw down the gun or I'll cock the trigger."

"And shoot me accidentally? Do you really want to spew my guts all over your barn? You probably wouldn't kill me, you know. I'd just lie here screaming and writhing on the floor. Think how long it'd take an ambulance to get here in this mess."

She seemed confused by his response, as if he wasn't quite what she'd been expecting.

"Tell you what," he offered. "I'll lay my gun on the feed bin over there if you'll do the same. I'm really not that crazy about having firearms pointed at me."

The woman paused.

"I'll even go first." He reached inside his jacket for his shoulder holster.

"Easy!" she warned.

"Nice and easy," he reassured her, slowly slipping the Magnum from its sheath.

Her eyes widened. Sweat beaded her brow as she monitored his every movement.

"Here we are." He held the gun by the nose, the grip pointed toward the floor. Taking two steps, the stranger settled the weapon on top of the feed bin.

"Now move away," she instructed. "And keep your hands raised above your head."

He did as she asked, walking toward the first stall,

and keeping his back to the barn door. "Your turn." He indicated the .22 with a wave of his head.

"Wrong."

"You agreed to put your gun down."

"I lied."

"Ah," he said, "the trustworthy type."

"Why should I trust you?"

"You shouldn't." He could tell by the look on her face she didn't know what to make of him.

"I think you better leave," she replied.

"You're going to throw me out in the freezing rain?" He saw indecision in the way she gnawed her bottom lip.

"I can't let you stay here."

"Why not?"

She swallowed hard. "I don't know anything about you."

"You're afraid. I understand. But if you let me sleep here, I'll be gone in the morning."

"For all I know you're an escaped murderer." Her words dropped into the silence, punctuated only by the sound of cows chewing and the milking machines whirling.

He raked his gaze over her body. She held herself ramrod stiff. They stared at each other, both leery, aware they were at an impasse. Her nostrils flared and he experienced a surge of sympathy. He had to let her off the hook, even if it meant freezing to death.

"All right," he said at last. "I'll go. Just let me get my duffel bag from the loft." He headed for the stairs, his heart turning over with despair at the thought of traipsing back out into the elements without his gun.

"Wait."

"What now?" Was she going to make him leave his duffel behind as well? He stopped and turned.

"I guess you can stay," she said. "But just until dawn and I'm taking your gun with me."

Her change of heart surprised and touched him. She was much braver than he'd originally given her credit for and kinder, too.

"Thank you, lady," he said, and meant it. "I appreciate the offer."

Wren studied the man before her, not really sure why she'd changed her mind. Something about him tugged at her. Something she couldn't quite put her finger on. Something that moved her deep inside.

He'd relinquished his weapon and then he'd been prepared to leave when she'd told him to go. That went a long way toward proving he meant her no harm. That, and the fact he'd taken the trouble to milk her cows.

"You're soaked to the skin," she said at last.

He shrugged and pushed a hand through dark unruly hair that curled about the collar of his black leather jacket. Water dripped from his clothing and pooled on the cement floor. The man emitted a very potent aura. She could almost feel his suffering. He was troubled and had been for a very long time. How she knew these things Wren couldn't say for sure, but know them she did.

A deep frown knitted his thick brows, forming a brooding V above his hawklike nose. His lips had been generously carved by nature but turned downward. That cynical expression, combined with several days' worth of beard growth, gave him an unsavory appearance. He might have been good-looking, she recognized, but the harshness in his eyes and the bitterness surrounding his mouth obscured whatever handsomeness had once graced those features.

Quiet loomed between them, thick and unyielding as the muddy landscape outside the window.

Letting him stay was probably very foolish, but truthfully what options did she have? Trapped by the storm, isolated without a phone, Wren was a virtual prisoner, at the mercy of this stranger's moods. Better to keep the upper hand by extending her hospitality, rather than turning him out, this time with a chip on his shoulder against her. Besides, it was almost Christmas and the man was a human being.

Do unto others. The phrase she strived to live by ran through her mind.

"I'm going to take your gun," she said. "And go back to the house. I'll bring you dry towels, blankets and something to eat."

"Thank you." Gratitude filled his voice and reassured her that she had chosen the right course.

She picked up the pistol from the feed bin. The safety was on and she tucked it into her coat pocket. "I'll be back in a few minutes. Why don't you get out of that wet coat?"

He nodded, his black eyes shining with something akin to respect.

Turning her back on him, she headed for the door, praying he wouldn't take advantage of her vulnerability and jump her from behind. She tried to minimize her limp, eager to hide her weakness. Her shoulders stayed stiff and rigid until she'd made it safely through the barn door.

The icy wind slapped her. Ducking her head against the onslaught, Wren saw that sleet coated the ground in a frosty white blanket and the stranger's gun weighed heavy in her pocket, banging against her tender hip as she walked.

Using care to navigate the precarious passage, Wren concentrated on placing one foot in front of the other, and tamped down the vision of the man she'd left behind. He was most definitely an enigma. Who was he, and what the heck was he doing in the middle of nowhere—in a raging winter storm—so close to Christmas, when most people were curled up safe and sound with their loved ones?

He's like you, the notion occurred to her. *He doesn't have any loved ones.*

How she knew that, Wren couldn't say. She simply knew it was true. Often, she got premonitions about people and events. She wasn't exactly psychic, she just got these feelings. In the past, when she ignored her internal urgings, something bad happened. Like with Blaine Thomas. At this moment, despite all outward appearances to the contrary, she felt that the stranger meant her no harm personally.

Wren shouldered the .22 and grasped the porch railing to steady herself as she mounted the steps. She burst through the door into the kitchen's warm, inviting embrace.

The radio played "Santa Claus Is Coming to Town." The pot of stew on the stove had grown cold but the hearty aroma lingered on the air. Wren laid the rifle across the table and placed the pistol beside it. She peeled off her gloves and coat and went to the kitchen. Flicking the burner on under the stew, she put a fresh pot of coffee on to percolate before heading down the hallway to the linen closet.

Extracting towels, sheets and blankets from the closet, she then carried them to the kitchen and packaged the bedding in a plastic garbage bag. While waiting for the stew to reheat and the coffee to brew, Wren leaned against the kitchen counter. The eight o'clock news came on. The weather forecast had worsened, with four inches of snow predicted. She shook her head in disbelief. It had been many years since such a fierce storm had swept through central Texas.

She squared her shoulders and filled one thermos with stew and a second with coffee. She sliced off a chunk of cranberry-walnut bread and slathered it with fresh butter before wrapping it in foil and tucking everything into a brown paper bag.

The return trip was trickier. She couldn't carry the rifle and the supplies, so she slipped the Magnum in her pocket and prayed it wouldn't be necessary for her to attempt to use the thing. The wind had died down but the walkway was even more treacherous now as the ice covered the ground with a thick glaze. Her ears stung and Wren wished she had remembered to put on a cap.

The barn door swung open before she reached it, the stranger silhouetted against the light. For a brief moment, he appeared like some dark archangel guiding her in from the cold.

"Smells wonderful," he said, closing the door behind her and rubbing his palms together in anticipation.

Wren discovered he had disconnected the cows from the milking machines while she was gone. She thanked him but he brushed aside her appreciation, reaching instead for the bundles she carried and setting them on top of the milk vat.

He'd removed his coat, she noted and he wore a long-sleeved black turtleneck sweater.

"Here." Wren reached inside the linen bag and

handed him a towel. He accepted it and began toweling his hair dry.

"I wondered if you were coming back," he said, tossing the towel aside and going for the food. An expression of pure joy crossed his face as he twisted open the thermos of stew and took a deep breath.

"Where else would I go?" Wren dug in the sack and handed him a spoon.

"You could have stayed in the house." He perched on a milking stool and plowed into the stew as if he hadn't eaten in weeks.

"I promised you food."

"A lot of people don't keep their promises, but I'm glad you did." He studied her intently. Wren gulped at the resulting heat from his penetrating stare. Twin fiery black diamonds drilled a hole straight through her. Something lurked behind his hooded expression. But what? He housed secrets. Wren saw twisted agony reflecting back at her. This man had experienced more than his share of sorrow.

"Do you work these cows alone?" He quirked an eyebrow at her over his spoon.

"My, er...husband will be back soon," she fibbed, self-preservation taking over.

"You don't have to lie to me," he said softly. "I know that you live alone."

"What makes you think I'm lying?"

"Your voice climbed an octave and you're fidgeting with your zipper." He pointed with his spoon.

Instantly, Wren stopped toying with her coat zipper.

"Don't worry," he said, "I'm not here to hurt you."

"What *are* you here for?" She startled herself by asking the question. If he was bent on harming her, what sort of answer would she have expected from him?

"Food." He waved at the thermos. "A place to sleep out of the weather. I have a little cash. I can pay for your hospitality. From the looks of this place, you could use the money." He settled a hand on his back pocket.

"That's not necessary." She shook her head. The man was a puzzle more intricate than the five-thousand-piece jigsaws she put together on long, lonely weekends.

"I don't want you thinking I'm a freeloader."

"I don't believe that."

"Why not?"

"You're different."

A wry expression crossed his face. "So are you. Most people would have sicced their dog after me."

"I don't have a dog, or I probably would have."

"Guess I'm lucky, then." He poured himself a cup of coffee and took a sip.

"Why are you on the road?" she asked, brushing a lock of damp hair from her forehead.

"Long story."

"Did your car break down?"

He swallowed, shook his head. "Back in Arizona. I've been hitchhiking ever since." He pulled a rumpled twenty from his pants pocket and laid it beside the paper bag.

"Keep your money." She raised her palms and rounded her shoulders beneath the weight of her down jacket.

"Are you sure?"

The man finished off the stew, put down his spoon and stared at her. Once again she was struck by his aura. It was a pure, physical presence. Strong emotions surrounded him, something very painful, something that tortured his soul. She could almost touch his suffering. Her fingers prickled inside her gloves.

"I'm sure."

He retrieved the twenty and Wren rattled in a shaky breath. People frequently made fun of her intuitive skills, but darn it, she *could* sense things about people that others never noticed.

He raised his head and in the harsh glare of light from the bare bulb, Wren saw a wicked, puckered scar running from behind his right ear down the length of his neck and disappearing into the collar of his shirt. A red, raw disfigurement that had taken many months to heal.

This man had been badly burned at one time. In a fire? she wondered. Or was it something else? Yes, he had suffered. Maybe as much as she herself had suffered.

A lurking danger smoldered deep within him. An internal darkness so strong Wren felt his pain to her very marrow. How mentally tortured was this man? Did he seek revenge on life for the damage to his skin? Had he taken to the road, his self-esteem shattered by a cruel twist of fate?

An empathetic pang zinged through her hip, as if on some cosmic level they shared the brotherhood of physical sorrow. She wanted to ask a million questions, but the look he gave her convinced Wren to bite her tongue.

He started in on the cranberry-walnut bread, making appreciative noises as he chewed.

"I'm Wren Matthews, what's your name?" she ventured, feeling like a first-grader.

He brushed crumbs from his fingertips, allowed his gaze to trail down her face and linger at her mouth. "Keegan Winslow," he said after a long pause.

Was he telling her the truth or had he concocted a name for her benefit? After all, the man was under no obligation to be forthcoming with her.

"Mr. Winslow." She knotted her hands together, curiosity capturing her. She stared pointedly at his burn. "What happened to you?"

"I prefer not to discuss my private life," he replied stiffly, slapping a palm over the scar in a useless attempt to disguise it.

What a vulnerable position she was in! She should be frightened by him, but oddly enough, he evoked her pity. Although Keegan Winslow was obviously a troubled man, she no longer felt threatened by him.

She didn't initiate any further conversation and to her surprise the hush that stretched between them was not an uncomfortable one. Wren liked that. She valued solitude.

His large hands were chapped raw by the rough weather, his fingernails cracked at the cuticles. His face had also suffered the effects of too much exposure to the elements. His skin was dry and fine wrinkles dug in around his eyes. He possessed the haggard look of a haunted soul. Or maybe he'd experienced something so sad, so tragic, he'd simply chosen to drop out of the mainstream and live life in the shadows.

Her empathy strengthened. She could understand that urge. She too, shied away from ordinary life, because of her deformity. She too, preferred seclusion. She too, was afraid to really risk again. It was far easier to hide from people, to cloak her emotions from the world.

Yes, she understood this man. He was alone, as she was. No immediate family to care for him on such a damp and lonely night. Angling her head, she observed him from the corner of her eye.

Keegan Winslow lifted his head and caught her inspecting him. His black eyes glimmered a warning. The look that passed between them was like a lightning bolt—quick and dangerous. She dropped her gaze to the floor.

The silence elongated, yawning wide as an endless chasm. It wasn't so comfortable now.

Thunder rumbled, distantly. Wren was surprised to discover her hands were shaking. She drew in a deep breath. Her wariness returned with a vengeance and suddenly she wanted to be back inside the house, far away from this mysterious man.

"You left the rifle behind." He observed.

"I've got your pistol in my pocket."

"Are you still afraid of me?" he asked.

"Who wouldn't be?"

"Smart girl." He leaned over to set the empty thermos on the stool and, straightening, his shoulder lightly grazed Wren's. She gasped at the intensity of her reaction to his touch. It was an odd sensation, similar to the feeling she'd experienced when she'd fallen off the playground swing as a six-year-old and knocked all the breath from her lungs.

"Are you all right?" He scrutinized her.

Wren nodded, not sure if she could even speak. Her tongue seemed welded to her palate. She inched away from him, hoping distance would dispel the commotion his touch had initiated. Her pulse leapt and her throat constricted. A portentous warmth spread throughout her body, warning her to be cautious.

Wren didn't know what to make of him. On the one hand, with his highly charged aura, he presented an inauspicious image. The picture of a man on the run. Unexpectedly, when she looked at him, Wren was reminded of that old television show, *The Fugitive*. Like the character in that series, Keegan appeared desperate and restless, as if frantically searching for his own one-armed foe.

The silence was back, punctuated only by the sounds of cattle chewing their cud.

Overhead, the sleet drummed steadily against the metal roof.

"It must get lonely out here, all by yourself," he said at last.

"I enjoy my privacy."

"Still, a woman alone in the wilderness. I hope you're serious about using that .22 if you're forced to." His words strummed a frightening chord.

Their eyes met.

"Yes," she said. "I wouldn't hesitate to protect myself."

"Good."

"If you don't need anything else, Mr. Winslow, I think I'll be going back to the house."

"Thanks for the food, Wren Matthews."

She frowned, more confused than ever. "I'd appreciate it if you were gone by morning."

He nodded. "Don't worry, I won't take advantage of your generous hospitality."

Wren let out her breath. She pulled on her gloves and headed toward the door.

"One more thing."

She looked up at him again. There was a severe expression on Keegan's face. The same sort of expression she'd seen on the cop that had attended the accident that had killed her parents and left her with a lifelong injury.

"Yes," she whispered, fear beading pearls of perspiration on her forehead.

"Always sleep with a gun under your bed and never trust anyone."

* * *

He should never have come here.

Keegan Winslow savored the last bite of Wren's homemade cranberry-walnut bread and washed it down with a swig of tepid coffee. Dusting his palms together, he sighed his pleasure. It was the best meal he'd had in recent memory.

A meal that strummed chords of home. A home that no longer existed. The sweetest of human comforts, lost to him forever.

Home. He didn't want to remember, but his mind refused to cooperate. Snippets of images flashed before his eyes. The savory stew, the soothing warmth, Wren Matthew's nervous smile, all conspired to evoke the past. A past he preferred to recall in the context of revenge, not the nostalgic sorrow of what had once been his.

The small brick cottage on the outskirts of Chicago. Two new vehicles in the garage. Vacations every summer, a roaring fireplace at Christmas time. Snowflakes and candy apples and crayon drawings posted on the refrigerator with magnets.

Gone. All gone. Slipped through his fingers and out of his life like smoke wisps. Sometimes he wondered if it had been a dream, if that old existence had ever been reality. These days hunger, pain and exhaustion seemed much more genuine than his short-lived happiness.

His childhood had prepared him for heartache. He'd been told often enough that life was tough and he had to be tougher. For the most part he'd believed that message. Until Maggie and Katie. For the briefest of time he'd inhabited a blissful world, ripe with possibilities, but then in the wink of an eye everything he cared about had been destroyed.

The dread that had lurked inside him for the last eighteen months rose like the monster it was and chewed at his innards. No, although his stomach was content, he most definitely shouldn't have stopped at this dairy. But he'd been desperate. Cold and wet and starving. Wren Matthews's farm had been a haven and Wren Matthews had been sight for road-weary eyes.

Not that the woman was a beauty. Not by any stretch of the imagination. Her features were much too plain, and she wore no makeup. But she had a presence about her. Something ethereal and otherworldly. A gentle soul among a sea of degenerates.

She offered him respite at a time when he needed it most. She reminded him too much of Maggie.

Yes. He most assuredly should not have lingered here.

In her quiet little world, he doubted if the woman had ever come into contact with a man like him.

Except for that limp.

He hadn't noticed it right away, he'd been so caught up in his own discomfort. She bore an old injury, he guessed, aggravated by the weather. Her physical imperfection heightened his curiosity. What had happened to her? Absentmindedly, Keegan fingered the old burn. The taut, stretched scar tissue still ached. He understood physical pain. That, he could handle. It was the emotional wounds he feared would never heal.

Running his tongue along his dry, weatherbeaten lips, he wondered about Wren living alone. It troubled him. Once upon a time, he had been as forward-thinking as the next person, and would not have found anything odd or unsafe about a woman running her own dairy. But now, Keegan felt differently. Women should be protected at all times. In his opinion, females should never live by themselves. The attitude was Neanderthal, he admitted it but he had his reasons.

Keegan knew he'd frightened her with his parting statement. But dammit, he wanted to warn her, without coming out and telling her the truth. Of course, now she believed him to be some sort of criminal. She'd been very foolish to even let him stay in her barn. The woman was an easy target for evil creatures—alone, vulnerable, exposed. But he couldn't deny he was grateful for her imprudence. If he'd spent much longer in the elements, he might have succumbed to pneumonia.

So much for Wren Matthews. By morning he would be gone, and hopefully the experience of coming into contact with him would have instilled caution in her.

Keegan stretched out on the cot and wrapped Wren's blanket around him. It smelled pleasantly of cotton and soap and a mild perfume. He pressed a corner of the blanket to his nose and inhaled. Lavender. He identified the aroma. He should have know she'd prefer such a scent—sweet, innocent, trusting.

Rolling onto his side, Keegan stared at the wall and listened to the rain and wind howling against the tin roof. Why was he thinking so fondly of this woman? For six months he'd considered nothing but retribution, and now, suddenly, he found himself wondering what it would be like to end his relentless searching, to stop seeking and settle down once more. To find comfort in loving arms.

No!

The word rose out of the darkness, harsh and bright. He'd lost the most precious thing a man could possess. He'd never place himself in such a precarious position again. Much better to spend the rest of his days bitter and lonely than to suffer such agony a second time.

Pressing his palms to his eyes, Keegan bit his tongue against the rising emotional tide. There would be no more happiness for him. Ever.

Chapter Three

The storm raged throughout the night.

Sleep came in fitful wakes and starts. Wren dozed, only to be awakened by vivid lightning slashing a path outside her bedroom window. Her nightgown was bathed in sweat and her pulse was pounding. She'd had a nightmare. An ugly dream in which unknown assailants were chasing her, and she'd been desperately searching for a gun.

Then Keegan Winslow's face had loomed in the darkness of her subconscious. She'd called out to him, begging for help. He'd come to her, his arms outstretched, but when he got close, she discovered he had her gun in his hands and was pointing it at her.

Wren lifted a trembling palm to her sweat-dampened temple and brushed back her bangs. Even in sleep she couldn't decide if the man was friend or foe.

Her sensible side urged wariness. He was a stranger and an ominous one at that. But something deep inside her, the instinctive part of her that had initially been suspicious of Blaine Thomas and his motives, trusted this man. Perhaps it was his burn scar that compelled her sympathy. Or maybe it was the sad, damned quality in his dark eyes. Whatever it was, he stirred her sensibilities. No matter how hard he tried to disguise it, Keegan Winslow was one of life's walking wounded.

She threw back the covers and got out of bed. Flicking on the lights as she went, Wren padded past the scraggly artificial Christmas tree she'd halfheartedly erected the day before. She'd hung several ornamental balls and twisted a few bows on the sparse limbs, but the overall affect was less than pleasing. She couldn't even say why she'd bothered. Maybe because even a fake tree with no presents beneath it was better than the loneliness of having no tree at all.

Shivering inside her housecoat, she turned up the thermostat before entering the kitchen. She wondered how Keegan Winslow had weathered the night. He must be freezing, even with the small space heater.

Curling her toes inside her thick woolen socks, she put on a pot of coffee, then cut a slice of cranberry-walnut bread and popped it in the microwave for half a minute. While she waited, she clicked on the radio to the farm report. The announcer was discussing pork futures.

Wren glanced at the clock. Five a.m. Time for milking.

In the barn. Alone. With Keegan Winslow.

If she stalled until dawn, the stranger might be gone. The cattle would be unhappy with her, but if she waited she wouldn't have to see the enigmatic stranger again.

You should offer the man breakfast for the road, her conscience goaded.

Yes, but that would mean she'd have to look into

those lonely eyes once more and see herself reflected there. Unnerved by that unsettling prospect, Wren pushed the thought away. Keegan Winslow was not her responsibility.

Everyone is your brother. Her preacher's gently chiding voice rattled around in her brain.

Wren went to the back door. She pushed it open a crack. Bitter cold immediately invaded the house, rough wind snaking in under the weather stripping. Her hip twinged in response. Switching on the porch lamp, she stared at the barn's shadowy shape.

No lights shone in the loft. Was the stranger still asleep?

The cement steps were slick with frost and icicles hung from the eaves. Shivering, Wren shut the door. She'd start a fire in the fireplace, have her breakfast and bath, get dressed and then reconsider her decision about postponing the milking until daylight.

Yawning, Wren took her cranberry-walnut bread from the microwave and spread butter over a hot yeasty slice. She poured a mug of coffee and liberally laced it with honey. Just what she needed, her daily jump start of sugar, fat and caffeine.

She sat down to eat, but guilt stabbed at her.

Here she was, warm and cozy, enjoying breakfast while Keegan Winslow was stuck inside that cold barn.

Wren sighed. This was exactly the reason she kept to herself. People simply complicated things. She didn't want to worry about the stranger. Heaven knew she had enough problems of her own.

Nevertheless, she couldn't shake the feeling of contrition—but the idea of inviting that silent, brooding male into her home had Wren shifting uncomfortably in her seat. What kind of person hitchhiked country back roads days before Christmas? A lonely one, obviously. Or maybe a dangerous one.

Her tummy quivered at the thought that he could be a lethal man. For all she knew he could be on the run from the law. He had to be fleeing something. Was his flight self-imposed or forced upon him by society's standards?

"Whatever it is, it's none of your concern, Wren Darlene Matthews," she scolded herself.

Despite her declaration, she was drawn to the barn and its human occupant. Curiosity warred against her natural reticence with people, men especially.

Getting up from her chair, Wren paced the floor, her housecoat swishing against her shins. Normally she possessed a calm, quiet steadiness of mind, not easily rattled even by her freshman students. But this morning agitation had her in its grip, and Keegan Winslow was at the root of her restlessness.

Her tender side urged her to help him.

Her fearful side warned her to stay inside with the doors securely locked.

Her tender side had landed her into big trouble before.

Her fearful side kept her withdrawn and isolated.

Wren stalked to the back door and peered out again. No change. The barn was dark but a hint of pink light hovered just above the horizon.

She could hear the cattle lowing in the barn. Their noises would only become more insistent. Surely Keegan Winslow could not continue to sleep through that din.

"Wait a little longer," she whispered to herself. "Go start a fire. Give him an hour to clear out. If he's not gone by six-thirty, you'll have to ask him to go."

Then a terrifying thought occurred to her. What if the stranger refused to leave?

Okay. Wren stared at her reflection in the toaster. To her own critical eye, she looked pale and owlish. Little sleep and a lot of worry had taken its toll. *No two ways about it. You've got to eject him from your barn.*

So what if it was ten degrees outside and two days before Christmas? She wasn't running a homeless shelter.

Resolutely, she pulled on her down jacket and jammed her feet into her boots. Wan sunlight fought with a thick cloud covering as she stepped onto the porch. Each time she exhaled, her breath billowed from her frosty lips like chugs of smoke. Wren shivered and trudged toward the barn, the frozen grass snapping and crunching beneath her rubber boots.

The cows mooed incessantly. She entered the barn and pulled the door shut tight behind her. She hesitated a moment, glancing around the stalls. The familiar smell of hay and milk and cow manure dominated the room.

Bossie bellowed, swished her tail and sent Wren a disgruntled expression.

"All right. I'm sorry," Wren apologized, still sweeping her gaze around the barn. No sign of Keegan Winslow. Perhaps she'd gotten lucky and he had left of his own accord. That thought lifted the anxiety from her shoulders and Wren stood a little straighter. "I deserve that disgusted look you're giving me." She reached over to scratch the knob on Bossy's head, her mind worrying over Keegan like a tongue at a sore tooth.

Maybe he's asleep in the loft.

How could he sleep through this commotion? she wondered, setting about her morning chores. As she worked, Wren cast frequent glances over her shoulder at the stairs leading to the loft, her ears straining for sounds of the stranger.

It took her three-quarters of an hour to connect all seventeen Holsteins to the milking machines. Once that task was completed, she limped to the bottom of the steps and stared up into the closed door.

She waited, fingers curled around the handrail, her heart racing in anticipation. After their odd exchange last night, Wren wasn't sure what to make of the man.

She cleared her throat. "Hello?" she called.

No answer.

"Mister Winslow?"

Was that a groan?

Wren titled her head. "Mister, are you all right?"

The creak of cot springs.

Why didn't he answer her?

Nervously, she chewed the inside of her cheek. She had no choice but to investigate. Hands trembling slightly, Wren put her foot on the bottom step.

The groan was louder this time.

Tentatively, Wren climbed the stairs. She reached the door, pushed it open, and peered into the airy loft.

A smudge of gray light drifted through the round window. Keegan Winslow lay curled into a fetal position on the cot, woolen blankets wrapped around him. Despite the space heater humming away in the corner the room was icy cold.

"Mr. Winslow?" She entered the loft and crept toward the bed. Was it a trap? A plan to lure her in, then attack?

He mumbled and thrashed about but his eyes remained closed. His breathing, Wren noted, was rapid and shallow.

She kept inching forward, body on full alert, ready to fling herself down the stairs if he should make an aggressive move. She silently cursed herself for leaving his pistol in the house.

The covers were wadded in his fists. He still wore his black jeans and turtleneck shirt, but his boots and his fedora lay under the bed.

Sweat beaded his brow and his lips were cracked and dry. Wren knelt beside him and reached out to touch his shoulder. "Mr. Winslow, it's morning. Time for you to leave."

His eyes flew open and he stared at something Wren could not see. Something terrifying.

"Maggie!" he cried and suddenly sat bolt upright in bed.

Startled, Wren tumbled backward, scrambling for the door. But just as quickly as he'd sprung to a sitting position, Keegan Winslow slumped back against his pillow.

Wren's pulse thudded a mile a minute. She gulped past the fear in her throat and stared at the man. His eyes were red-rimmed and glassy with a feverish shine.

She hung back, her hand pressed to her chest. Who was Maggie? she wondered. And what was wrong with Keegan Winslow?

"Mr. Winslow," she whispered. "Are you awake?"

He didn't reply, just stared grimly at the ceiling.

Wren edged closer. Was he asleep with his eyes open?

A gust of wind blew through the cracks, sending a chill down Wren's spine. She burrowed deeper into the folds of her down coat and squatted beside the cot once more.

His eyelids had shuttered closed again. Wren stripped off her glove and laid a hand across his forehead.

The man was burning with fever!

"Keegan?" she asked, using his first name.

He looked at her and blinked. "Who are you?" he croaked, his voice hoarse. His skin was very dry, signaling dehydration. She had to get water into him and soon.

"My name's Wren Matthews, Mr. Winslow. Do you remember spending the night in my barn?"

He shook his head and looked so forlorn the expression twisted her heart.

"You've got a high fever. I'm going to get you some water. Are you cold?"

In answer, his teeth chattered and he drew the blankets more tightly around him.

"Sit tight. I'll be right back," Wren fretted. She hurried down the stairs and through the barn. She bent her head against the frigid blast that greeted her and scurried to the house.

You're going to have to bring him inside the house, the thought occurred to her. *He's too sick to stay in the cold, drafty loft.*

The notion nagged at her. It was foolhardy bringing an unknown man into her home, but oddly enough, perhaps because of his illness, perhaps because of the desolate way he'd called that woman's name, Wren was no longer frightened of Keegan Winslow. He was a man in need of help and she had always had a hard time turning away from anyone in trouble.

Wren poured a bottle of water, retrieved one of her father's heavy winter coats from the hall closet and returned to the barn. She found Keegan in the same position she'd left him in.

"I'm back," she said, perching on the cot's edge. She twisted the lid from the water bottle and held it in her right hand. Her hip brushed against his thigh. She sucked in a breath at the contact. Even through several layers of material she could feel the delineation of his muscles. Her immediate reaction was swift and unmistakable— even in his incapacitated state the man aroused her!

Nervously, she stared at him, darting quick glances over the length of his body. Never had she experienced such a strong, instant connection to anyone. Much less a total stranger.

He mumbled something unintelligible.

"Here." Wren ran her left hand under his pillow and raised his head. Her fingers sank into the soft goose feathers. His dark hair provided a stark contrast against the white pillowcase and his eyes appeared hollow in his gaunt face. "Take a sip."

He groaned.

"Open your eyes."

His eyelashes fluttered and he stared up at her. "Angel," he murmured.

She placed the bottle beneath his chapped lips. "Drink."

He did as she asked, drinking thirstily until he'd emptied the bottle. When he had finished, Wren eased his head down onto the cot.

"Thank you."

His gratitude touched her more than she cared to admit. Strange feelings surged through her. Feelings she should not be experiencing toward a lonely hitchhiker.

"We need to get you into the house."

"House?" He gave her a quizzical look. "Where are we now?"

"In my barn."

"I thought I smelled cow manure." He wrinkled his nose.

"Can you walk, Mr. Winslow?"

"Of course I can walk." He sounded irritable.

"You're very weak."

He waved a hand. "Point me in the direction."

"Why don't we start with letting you sit on the side of the bed?"

"Good idea."

His dark eyes glistened and Wren realized the man was probably delirious. Was moving him at this juncture such a great idea? She couldn't say.

"Help me up," he insisted.

He reached out his hand to her and she took it. His skin was blistering hot. Worried, Wren frowned. His temperature had to be at least a hundred and two, maybe higher. He should see a doctor.

"Upsadaisy," she said and tugged him to a sitting position.

He swung his legs over the cot, then sat there a moment, breathing heavily and clutching his head.

"You okay?"

"Dizzy."

Keegan closed his eyes and leaned so far over, she feared he'd topple onto the floor.

Why am I doing this? Wren wondered. *He's nothing to me but trouble.*

Because he was in need. Because it was two days before Christmas and because on some subterranean level, she related to this man and his suffering. And because, if Wren dared admit it, she was wildly attracted to him with an intensity that shocked and surprised her.

"Here." She reached for her father's overcoat and held it out to him. "Stick your hand in."

Like a two-year-old being dressed by his mother, Keegan followed her command, sluggishly poking his arms through the sleeves.

"Boots next."

He lifted his feet, first one and then the other, and allowed her to guide him into his boots.

"There." She rocked back on her heels to assess his condition. He looked awfully pale.

"Okay," he said, faintly. "Let's try it."

"Are you sure?" She puckered her lips in concern.

He nodded. "Yeah."

"Brace yourself against me," she instructed, wrapping an arm around his waist and assisting him to stand.

He swayed like a slender poplar in the wind. The top of Wren's head came level with his shoulder and she noticed he smelled surprisingly clean. That realization heightened her curiosity. Obviously, the man bathed regularly.

Who was Mr. Keegan Winslow? She pondered the question. He fit the profile of neither a criminal nor an indigent. His leather jacket, though worn, was of top quality. Likewise his boots. From what little he'd said the night before, she knew his vocabulary was that of an educated person. Everything about him was contradictory, from his secretive demeanor to the fact he'd milked her cows the night before. Wren, with her limited experience of the opposite sex, hardly knew what to make of this masculine creature that had come to roost in her loft.

"Where do we go from here?" he asked.

"We've got to make it down those stairs." She pointed to the flimsy ladder extending to the barn below.

"Which one?" He squinted.

"What do you mean?"

"The stairs on the right or the stairs on the left?"

Wren suppressed a groan. He had double vision. Perhaps the most prudent course of action would be to ease him back down on the bed and forget the whole thing. But as that thought occurred to her, a gust of wind rattled the barn and slipped glacial talons through the uninsulated cracks. The barn might be warm enough for cattle, but the loft was definitely too cold for a man with a fever. Besides, it would be hard for her to keep a watchful eye on him so far removed from the house.

"Follow me," she instructed.

He placed large palms on her shoulders and braced himself against her. She took a backward step toward the door and the steep flight of stairs beyond it. He shuffled along after her. The result was a bizarre, uncoordinated dance. Step, one, two, slide.

She paused every moment or two to let him catch his breath and battle the dizziness. His face turned pink with effort and perspiration pearled on his upper lip.

Keegan's belt buckle grazed her rib cage. His fingers clung to her shoulders for support. He misstepped a time or two and came down on her toes.

"Sorry," he mumbled.

"Don't worry about it."

Suddenly, he no longer looked like the scruffy outlaw who'd barged into her barn. Instead, he seemed like a lost little boy, tired, weary and searching for home. A tenderness unfolded inside Wren and she resisted the desire to brush a lock of errant hair from his forehead and give him a big, reassuring hug.

"You're doing fine," she encouraged.

"Liar."

"We're almost to the stairs." When Wren's foot moved out over the top step, she faltered. Now for the hard part.

"Mr. Winslow," she said, "we've got to go down these steps. Can you make it?"

"Uh," he grunted. "Can't."

"What's wrong?" She looked into his face, saw sheer exhaustion reflected there.

"Legs won't move."

Oh, dear. Before she had a chance to consider her plight, Keegan Winslow's knees telescoped beneath him and he fell past her, right down the stairs, and hit the barn floor below.

"Mister Winslow, speak to me, please."

Keegan blinked at the brown-haired waif leaning over him. His head hurt like hell and his vision was blurry. He felt hot and sluggish and he wished the woman would stop bobbing around him like a worried hen with a lost chick. She leaned in close and for the briefest of moments, he mistook her for someone else.

"Maggie?" he croaked, knowing even as he said the name, that she wasn't Maggie.

"No, I'm Wren. Wren Matthews."

"Ah."

"Is Maggie your wife?"

Keegan winced. "Was."

Sympathy flitted across her face and Keegan had to bite down on his tongue to stay the anger rising inside him. He was sick of pity, especially from strangers. Sick of people who pretended to know what it was like to lose someone. Sick of misguided do-gooders. This damned girl had no idea of the anguish he'd endured.

"You're bleeding!" she exclaimed.

He put a hand to the back of his head and it came away sticky. He tried to sit up, but she firmly pushed him back down and pulled a handkerchief from her pocket. Squatting beside him, she pressed the cloth to his scalp.

How old-fashioned, he thought vaguely, *to carry a handkerchief.*

"Don't move," she cautioned, her fingers touched his skin and created a soothing balm in the sea of pain.

"Why not?"

"You've got a head injury."

"Oh." He supposed that was why she looked so panic-stricken. What he couldn't figure out was why she cared. Who was she? "What happened to me?"

"You don't remember?"

"Nothing past last night."

"You woke up sick this morning. Feverish, dizzy, weak. I think you've got the flu or something. I tried to get you into the house but you fell down the stairs from the loft."

She pointed upward and Keegan's eyes widened when he realized he'd tumbled a good eight feet right onto his noggin. No wonder he couldn't remember anything.

"You could have a concussion or worse," she fretted.

Keegan propped himself up on one elbow and watched her. The woman was attractive in a quiet, understated way. Personally, he'd never gone in for flashy women.

"What's the matter?"

She raised an eyebrow. "Matter?"

"You're limping."

She shook her head as if the limp were a mere nuisance. "It's nothing. An old injury."

He got to his knees.

"What are you doing?" she exclaimed.

"Getting up."

"That's how you got hurt in the first place!"

"Well, I can't lie here all day, now, can I?" he snapped.

Keegan used a stall door to steady himself. A wide-eyed Holstein stared at him, then swished her tail in dismissal. He frowned and tried to think. His mouth was incredibly dry and alternating waves of heat and cold washed over him.

"If you insist on getting up, then let's try to make it to the house," she suggested.

On this point, Keegan was inclined to agree with her. He had a desperate longing for a soft warm bed.

"Lean on me." She offered her body as support.

Against his better judgment, Keegan took her arm and instantly regretted it. The sensation rushing through him was intense and overwhelming. Sudden need filled him. A need to put his head in her lap and let her stroke her fingers through his hair until all his worries and fears evaporated. A need to embrace her warm, loving being and lose himself there. It was a sensation he hadn't felt in a very long time and it spelled nothing but trouble for both him and this kind woman.

It's the fever, Keegan told himself. *That and nothing more.*

He kept his eyes downcast, hoping she wouldn't see the neediness on his face. Concentrating, he focused on putting one foot in front of the other and denying the emotions she stirred within him.

"Not much farther," she whispered, her voice as soft as the expression in her eyes and he found himself wondering what he'd done to deserve such an angel.

A mere two hours ago her goal had been to remove this man from her premises, now she was praying to get him into her house without further problems.

Dried blood clung to the back of his head, and his jeans were ripped across one knee. He leaned heavily against her but she could tell it irked him to have to depend on her for support. She propped him against a stall while she opened the barn door. The thrust of cold air that shot into the room sent him into a coughing fit.

Wren pressed her lips into a tense line. He should be seen by a doctor. She said as much.

"No," Keegan replied harshly. "No doctors."

"But you're ill."

"I'll live." He said the words as if living were a bad thing.

Was it because of his wife? Wren wondered. Had losing her robbed him of his will to live? Was he widowed or divorced? A gush of sympathy washed through her. Curious emotions crowded in on her. Emotions she didn't want to examine. When he'd lain on the barn floor looking up at her, the oddest expression had crossed his face. As if he'd actually found her desirable.

Fat chance, her internal naysayer scoffed. Who would find a crippled woman sexually desirable? She wasn't whole, she'd always be lacking. Blaine Thomas had held that ugly mirror before her face. And what if Winslow did find her attractive? Good heavens, for all she knew he was a criminal. Yet something told her that deep inside, Keegan Winslow was an honest and decent man who'd fallen on hard times. Apparently, he had seen the raw, ugly side of life and had lived to tell the tale. Nevertheless, she wasn't about to let herself entertain any sort of romantic notions about this man.

What was wrong with her for even considering such thoughts? Why did her body respond so vigorously to him. Was she that desperate? Had she been so isolated for so long that she'd forgotten Blaine Thomas's valuable lesson?

They left the barn and started across the yard. Keegan's foot hit an icy patch and he slipped, barely maintaining his balance.

"Easy." Wren steadied him and they continued their progress over the frozen ground.

White smoke plumed gently from her chimney and the scent of wood smoke lingered in the air. The grass cracked beneath their feet like sharp gasps. Icicles hung from tree branches and off the house eaves. The Christmas-tree lights she'd strung on the fence a week after Thanksgiving looked bare and lonely against the gray background.

"Not much farther now," she promised, guiding him up the porch and into the house. Wren shut the door behind them and a heavy silence descended. She glanced up to see him staring at her.

"Thank you," he whispered, his voice thick and husky. He grasped the back of a kitchen chair.

"You're welcome."

"I feel so stupid."

"There's nothing to be ashamed about. Everyone gets sick. Once you've had some sleep you'll feel better," she reassured him. It was hard to believe that last night she'd been terrified of this man who now appeared so sad and forlorn. "Can you make it just a little farther?"

He nodded.

She led him down the corridor to the bedroom that had once belonged to her parents. While he sat down in a chair and pulled off his boots, Wren turned back the covers and fluffed the pillow.

"There." She turned around to find Keegan slumped

against the wall. "Oh my gosh." She leapt to his side. "Are you all right?"

"No strength. Feel like a damned fool."

"Shhh. It's okay." She knelt before him and pried off his boots. "Stand up."

Groaning, he obeyed.

As if she did this every day, Wren's fingers deftly unbuckled his belt. She tried not to think of the sexual connotations, just kept reminded herself Keegan was ill and needed her help. It was no different than if she were a nurse.

Yet her hand hesitated at his zipper.

A lump rose in her throat and her cheeks flamed with embarrassment. Could she do this?

He swayed and she thought he was about to topple over again. That spurred her into action. She tugged the zipper down, and with both hands grasped the waistband and pulled his trousers to his knees.

Her breath caught in her windpipe at the sight of his bare body. She'd only had occasion to see one naked man and Keegan Winslow put Blaine Thomas to shame with his washboard belly and the thatch of dark hair that trailed past the waistband of his jeans.

"Can you step out of your pants?" she squeaked. He nodded and together they managed to shuck his blue jeans over his feet. Keegan sat there in his boxer shorts and she tried her best not to stare at his finely chiseled physique.

"Hands up," Wren said.

"Huh?"

"Raise your hands over your head so I can get your shirt off."

Keegan raised his hands for her. A tenderness she'd never felt before descended upon Wren. Standing on tiptoe in order to reach high enough, she caught hold of his shirttail and lifted the garment over his head.

The burn scar that started at this neck widened across his broad back, disfiguring his handsome body, but instead of repulsing her, the injury stirred her sympathy. Her hand was drawn to it, like a magnet. Tenderly, she reached out and grazed her fingertips over the wound.

"Don't," he said sharply.

Wren snatched back her hand and cradled it against her chest.

"I'm sorry," she apologized. "I had no right to touch you."

The man said nothing. She peeked at his face. His eyes were closed, his lips pressed firmly together.

"Come," she said, "lie down."

He moved toward the bed, her heart lurching with each stumbling step. Why did she ache so to see him in such misery? Why did her hip twinge in sympathy at the sight of his ravaged back? Why did she long to reach out to him?

Keegan settled onto the mattress then allowed his lean frame to be enveloped by the plump bedding. Wren pulled the comforter over him and he groggily muttered his appreciation.

Wren crept into the hallway, tugging the door closed after her. Hands behind her back, she leaned against the wall, fighting the myriad of sensations swirling within.

Just who was this mysterious stranger sleeping in her bed?

Chapter Four

Returning to the barn to finish her chores, Wren discovered she could not stop thinking about Keegan Winslow. As she scooped muck from the stalls, then added fresh straw, she kept seeing his troubled face dance before her eyes.

She was attracted to him, there was no denying it. He caused her pulse to race, her heart to thump faster in her chest, her stomach to squeeze into a hard, tight knot. She didn't know if it was his dangerous, bad-boy mien or the scarred desolate quality that hung about him, but she found the man recklessly intriguing.

And that fact was downright scary.

If he was on the run from the law, she was courting trouble simply harboring him here. If on the other hand he was mentally tortured, crippled emotionally by whatever had disfigured his body, she needed to give him an even wider berth. She couldn't heal him. So often women made the mistake of thinking they could change a man. Wren had discovered the hard way such transformations had to come from within the person. No external force, no concerned individual, no undying love could straighten a twisted soul.

But maybe Mr. Winslow had compelling reasons for hitchhiking the countryside, she argued with herself. Reasons that if known, would explain his behavior.

Don't, her conscience warned but she couldn't seem to dispel her thoughts. She wanted Keegan to be more than an aimless drifter or a shell-shocked mental case.

But why? It wasn't as if she needed a man. She got along perfectly well on her own. Sure, she was lonesome on occasion, but who wasn't? Goodness, why was she even fantasizing about the likes of this stranger? That fact told a sorry tale about her self-esteem. Just because she was shy and crippled didn't mean she was desperate enough to settle for the first ragtag refugee who popped up on her doorstep.

Wren stopped to rest, leaning on the handle of her shovel for support. She was slightly out of breath from exertion, and her hip ached. She might not need a man in the romantic sense, but she certainly needed someone to help run the dairy.

But what if...? No. Wren tossed her head. It was a very stupid idea.

Bossie switched her tail, swatting Wren's arm and creating a crinkling noise against the sleeve of her down coat. Wren reached out a hand and affectionately patted the cow's hindquarters. "Hey there, old heifer, still mad at me from last night?"

Lowering her head, Bossie let out an accusatory moo.

"Yeah, well, I'm sorry, but the circumstances were beyond my control," she apologized.

Bossie blinked her wide brown eyes and snorted.

Wren grinned. At times, Bossie seemed almost human. Actually, Keegan had done a darned fine job of milking the cows last night. Speculatively, Wren nibbled her bottom lip. She'd be foolish to offer Keegan a job as her farmhand. She knew nothing of the man, save his name, and even that might be fictional.

It wasn't as if he'd be the first man to lie to her.

Except this was different. She pitied Keegan and wanted to help him. This wasn't at all like that time with Blaine.

She tried to squelch the memory, but it rose up anyway. Even though ten years had passed, her shame was as vivid and painful as if it had happened yesterday.

Blaine Thomas had driven into her driveway one hot summer afternoon in his bright red Mustang convertible. She had been weeding her garden and at the first sight of him, she had been tempted to plunge into the corn rows and hide until he left. But he had already seen her and was climbing out of his car.

"Howdy!" he called out, stalking across the yard with a purposeful stride. "How you doing? I'm Blaine Thomas."

He talked so fast and with such animated gestures, Wren had been taken aback. She'd stood in the garden, her mouth hanging open in awe, her hoe clutched in her hand. Her straw hat was cocked back on her head and she knew she had dirt streaked across one cheek but that didn't seem to deter him any.

There was no denying Blaine was an eye-catching specimen, with his thick blond hair and tall athletic build.

"C...c...can I help you?" she'd stammered, flustered as a novice teacher on her first day as a substitute.

The roving assessment he'd given her had sent a hot flush running up her neck so fast and furious Wren had wondered if she might be experiencing heatstroke. No man had ever looked at her as if he wanted to lick her like an ice-cream cone.

"Yes, ma'am, you certainly can." He'd walked right over to her and offered his palm. She'd been so stunned, so socially inept, it never occurred to her to shake his hand.

Blaine hadn't missed a beat, he'd merely swept his hand up to rest it on her shoulder. That foreign touch had made her cringe but she'd been so overwhelmed she'd said nothing. His handsomeness had made her uneasy from the start—as if a man that good-looking could be interested in a woman like her! Wren should have listened to that little voice, but alas, she had ignored her inner urgings in favor of her pathetic need to ease her loneliness.

"They told me you were a good, reliable person, but I had no idea you'd be so pretty and so fetching," he said in a soft, flattering tone.

"They?"

"Reverend Duvall and those kind ladies from the East Side Baptist Church."

She'd relaxed at the mention of Reverend Duvall's name. If her pastor had directed his man out here, surely she could let down her guard. "Reverend Duvall sent you?"

"Yes, ma'am, when I told him I was looking for a Holstein calf, he told me you had one for sale."

"Actually, I've got several."

That had been in the days when she'd had a herd of over eighty head of cattle and two employees. Back before Blaine had cleaned her out. Wren gritted her teeth against the memory. She'd been such a simpering fool.

And having been burned once she'd be an even bigger

fool to give Keegan Winslow a chance at taking what little remained of her once-thriving dairy.

Bossie mooed again, snapping Wren from her reverie. Time to put away her tools and head back to the house to check on her patient, but first she'd collect Keegan's things from the loft.

She hosed off the shovel and hung it from a peg on the wall. Stripping off her work gloves, she stuffed them into her pocket before ascending the stairs.

The loft remained bitingly cold. Good thing she'd removed Keegan from here. He might not have survived the weather with his fever. She swept her gaze around the room. Keegan's brown fedora lay beneath the cot, his leather jacket in a heap on the floor.

Wren squatted beside the bed and picked up the felt hat. Fingering it lightly, she placed it on her own head. It was too big and the brim dipped low over her forehead. She felt like that girl in the shirt commercial raiding her absent husband's closet for the smell and feel of him. Unsettled by that inappropriately intimate thought, she doffed the hat and tucked it under her arm.

His duffel sat in the wicker chair that had one leg shorter than the other three. Wren rose to her feet, plucked the bag from the chair and shouldered it. She bent to scoop up the jacket. When she draped the garment over her arm, Keegan's scent wafted around her. It was a masculine aroma. Warm and comforting.

Wren shook her head. She had to stop these thoughts. The fluttery feeling in her stomach, the tightness in her chest worried her. These sensations had gotten her into trouble before, and although Wren knew it wasn't right to compare Keegan with Blaine, neither could she allow hormones and a misguided sense of duty to lead her down the wrong path. Keegan was a stranger and a forbidding one at that. Just because she was attracted to his smell, just because his sad expression stirred something inside her did not mean she had to act on those feelings.

Turning on her heels, she started for the stairs. As she swung around, something fell from the duffel bag's side pocket and drifted to the floor. From her peripheral vision, Wren caught sight of it. Stepping backward, she took a second look.

It was a photograph.

Letting the jacket, hat and duffel slide to the ground, she leaned over and reached out to pick up the picture.

Its edges were curled. Fingerprints and waterstains marred the glossy finish.

Wren sucked in her breath and studied the people depicted there. A family. Man, woman and child.

The man had to be Keegan. Same build, same features, same coal-dark hair.

But he looked so different. His face was an open book. His eyes housed no secrets, his mouth turned upward in a radiant smile. Instead of appearing gaunt and drawn, he was muscular and broad. He wore shorts, a polo shirt and a gold band on his ring finger.

His hair was cut short, the way a military man or police officer might wear it. Could he have once been a soldier or a cop? That gave her pause. He seemed the type. Strong, controlled, guarded and silent. She rubbed a finger over his face. Most telling of all, the scar on his neck was absent in this picture.

He had one arm draped casually across the woman's shoulder. She was looking at him as if the sun shone from his eyes. She was laughing, open mouth. She was pretty, but not gorgeous. Her eyes were too wide, her mouth too generous. She had beautiful, shimmering shoulder-length blond hair, caught up in a bright blue bow. She wore a simple flower-print housedress, exactly the sort of garment Wren preferred, and white sandals adorned her feet.

In her arms, the woman clutched a baby. Probably about a year old. The child was dressed in a pink pinafore, so Wren assumed it was a girl. She looked like her mother, blond and fair.

They were outside somewhere, a lush green field with lots of trees in the background.

How old was the photograph? Wren wondered, flipping it over but finding no date on the back.

Obviously this was Keegan's wife and daughter. But what had happened to them? Were they dead or alive? She shuddered and her heart wrenched. Oh, the poor man. What losses he must have suffered. Perhaps even worse than her own. Tears welled in Wren's eyes and she knew what she had to do.

No matter her doubts and her fears, this felt right. Keegan needed a place to stay and she'd wished for someone to help her farm the dairy. It was as if heaven had dropped him into her lap. Tucking the photograph back in the duffel and collecting his things once more, Wren made up her mind. She would ask him to stay.

Opening his eyes, Keegan stared at the ceiling. Where in the hell was he?

His head hurt. Badly. He was so thirsty his lips were stuck together. And he was cold. Damned cold. He shivered. Looking down, he saw he was wrapped in at least three blankets and a fluffy lace comforter. Why was he so cold?

He swept his gaze around the room. Antiques. Lots of them. A highboy sat to one side, with a cobalt vase perched atop it. Homey landscape oil paintings adorned the walls and the windows were covered with white lace curtains that matched the comforter.

How had he gotten here?

Keegan lifted his head off the pillow but was immediately assailed with vicious dizziness. Groaning, he eased himself back down and rested an arm across his throbbing head.

Think, Winslow. Think.

He closed his eyes and took a deep breath. It hurt and set off a paroxysm of coughing.

Keegan pulled the covers over his head, curled into a ball and rode out the spell, his whole body racked with the force.

The door creaked.

"Keegan?" the voice was a low whisper.

Maggie? His heart lurched hopefully but something nagged at him that it couldn't be so. He peeled back the covers and peeked out.

A slender woman stood silhouetted in the light from the hallway. She wore an apron and smelled of apple pie. Just like Maggie.

He blinked. His vision was blurry and he didn't trust what he was seeing. Could it be true? Was Maggie alive after all?

Stunned, his feverish mind tried to process the information but he couldn't think.

"I've got juice and aspirin," she said, moving into the room, bringing her delicious scent with her and the sound of ice tinkling in a glass. "How are you feeling?" The woman's voice was soft and melodious. Like his Maggie's. Except she spoke with a Southern accent and Maggie was from Nebraska.

He tried to answer and was startled to hear his word come out harsh and gravelly. "Thirsty," he rasped.

She moved to the side of the bed and slipped her hand under his head. Like a mother tending a child, she lifted him up. "Open your mouth."

Obediently, he opened his mouth and she dropped two pills on his tongue, then placed the rim of the cool glass against his lips.

"Swallow."

He washed down the pills and practically inhaled the apple juice. "Thank you," he whispered.

"You're welcome."

She started to move away but he reached out and grasped her hand. She tensed at his touch. Was she afraid of him? Keegan hoped not. He had to let her know how grateful he was for her kindness.

He gripped her hand tightly and raised it to his lips. She felt so soft, so smooth, so young and full of life. Tenderly, he kissed that hand, his lips brushing her skin, once, twice, three times before she gently extricated herself and limped out the door.

Simply touching her had a profound effect on him. Instantly, he was soothed. Keegan fell asleep at the same time he realized his mysterious nurse was not his beloved Maggie.

Startled, Wren stumbled to the living room and dropped onto the couch. Her hand tingled from Keegan's touch and her stomach rode a crazy roller coaster.

She was scared. Very scared. She should not be feeling like this, and yet she was.

Clenching her fists and biting her lip, Wren stared out the window at the gray clouds merging thickly on the horizon. She couldn't believe the overwhelming effect the stranger's lips had created, just by lightly brushing the back of her hand. The kiss couldn't have been more powerful if it had been on the lips, openmouthed, with tongues entwined.

She knew there had been nothing sexual in it, no invitation, no secret awareness. Keegan Winslow had simply been grateful for her care. She knew that and yet she couldn't halt the emotions stampeding through her body.

She experienced so many conflicting sensations when she gazed upon him. Empathy, sadness, trepidation, excitement. And need. Yes, the sharp aching need a woman has for a man. She longed to reach out to him. To touch him, to soothe and comfort this odd stranger who'd suffered so much in his short life.

"You can't allow yourself to feel anything for this man, Wren," she whispered. "Even if he's not what he appeared to be at first, he can only hurt you. He's here today and gone tomorrow. Besides what would he want with a lame spinster?"

Wren clenched her jaw as she thought about the hurtful accusation Blaine had flung at her when she'd discovered he was stealing from her and she'd confronted him. He'd told her she was ugly and pitiful. That no man would ever want such a pathetic cripple.

And she'd believed him.

Shaking her head to dispel the memory, Wren got up and went to the kitchen. She'd make the stranger a pot of chicken noodle soup. Nothing was as healing as the vitamin-packed combination of chicken, celery, carrots, onions and pasta. She'd minister to this sick man as God had obviously intended for her to do and then she'd set him free. Offering him the job as farmhand was too risky. Her feelings for him tempted fate.

Just get him on his feet and send him on his way. She could hold herself in check for a day or two. She'd maintain a polite but distant manner, and then he'd be gone and she'd never have to see or worry about him again. It wasn't as if that would be hard. The stranger didn't seem eager to become involved with her, any more than she was with him.

Wren exhaled deeply. Fine. That was settled. But no matter how hard she scrubbed her hands at the kitchen sink, she couldn't wash away the invisible imprint his lips had branded upon her hand.

The second time he woke, Keegan felt much better, even though he was bathed in sweat. He threw aside the covers and tried to sit up but his body was so damned weak. Giving up the struggle, Keegan turned on his side.

There was a knock at the door.

"Come in," he said, surprised to discover how much energy it took to say those two words.

The door eased open and timidly the woman stepped into the room. He'd forgotten her name. Keegan frowned. Why was he thinking of birds? Robin? Was that her name? No. That wasn't it. He remembered that the name suited her. Wren. That was it. A little brown wren.

"You're soaked," she said, sinking her hands on her hips and appraising him.

Was it his imagination or did her eyes linger on his bare chest? Self-consciously, Keegan covered himself with his hands.

"At least you're fever's broken, but we've got to get you cleaned up and get some dry linens on your bed." She spoke matter-of-factly, as if he wasn't almost naked in the bed. "Do you think you could make it to the chair? You could give yourself a sponge bath while I change your sheets."

"Yeah."

''Here, put your arm around my shoulder.''

Feeling like a helpless fool, he did as she said, gingerly swinging his legs off the bed at the same time. He didn't like being this close to her, this dependent on her kindness. It was too cozy, too intimate, too much like man and wife.

Slowly, they made it the few short feet to the straightbacked chair near the window. Keegan sank down like a stone, uncomfortably aware he had nothing on but his boxer shorts.

As if sensing his thoughts, Wren stripped a light blanket from the bed and draped it around him. He saw her lips tighten as she stared at his burn scar. Keegan swallowed. That ought to scare her off.

''I'll be right back,'' she said, then disappeared.

He took a deep breath and blinked against the cottony feeling stuffing his head. He had no idea what time it was or for that matter, what day. He peered out the window and saw a sheet of ice coating the ground. The sky was dark but it was still daylight. Sometime in the late afternoon, he judged.

''Here we are,'' Wren said with false brightness. She carried a basin, soap, washrag and towel.

Keegan had been in enough hospitals to know how caretakers operated. ''You don't have to cheer me up,'' he said. ''I feel like hell and I'm sure I look twice as bad.''

''You're nothing to write home about,'' she agreed and the quick glimpse of her humor surprised him. He gave a halfhearted grin. She sat the basin down on the table next to him, dropped in the washrag and soap.

Wren turned her back on him and leaned over the bed to peel the fitted sheet from the corner of the mattress. Keegan honestly didn't mean to notice but it was hard to miss the way her blue jeans fit perfectly against her heart-shaped bottom, the way her pink shirt complemented her smooth complexion. He admired her light brown hair curling about her shoulders and the way her body swayed when she moved.

There was something about her that demanded his attention even though she wasn't classically beautiful, and she walked with a limp. No. It was more than her appearance that drew him to her. She possessed a certain quality that one rarely saw in this day and age. Wren Matthews was a throwback to a gentler time. She was quiet and sweet-natured, but with a thread of pure steel running through her. He recalled the night before, and her shaky threat that she was going to shoot first and ask questions later if he didn't come down from the loft.

Remembering, Keegan felt a peculiar stirring in his gut. A sensation he was afraid to name.

What was wrong with him? Why was he thinking like this? Not once in the eighteen months since Maggie's death had he even thought about another woman, much less suffered from sexual arousal. Why now? Why Wren?

Turning his head to drive out the rampant thoughts crashing through his brain, Keegan dipped his hand into the warm water, retrieving the soap and washrag.

Wren Matthews was an unusual lady. Not too many solitary women would have taken him into their home, much less offered him nursing care. He wasn't complaining. Keegan had been in dire need of a little TLC. Problem was, he could get used to this. Real easily, and he could not, under any circumstances, allow that to happen.

Why couldn't he have landed in the home of an elderly woman, or a boisterous family, or a solitary bach-

elor? Why had he been cursed and delivered into the
arms of a tenderhearted young woman? Then again, why
not? His bad luck just kept getting worse. In the last
eighteen months, he could have given Job a run for his
money.

Keegan washed his face, his neck, his arms and was
surprised to find himself out of breath. He leaned against
the back of the chair and tried not to pant.

Apparently the last six months had caught up with
him. Too little sleep, too little food, too much physical
exertion had brought his body down with a vengeance.
And he hated it. This vulnerability. How could he continue his quest until he could walk without stumbling?
How could he hope to challenge his nemesis if he wasn't
strong enough to hold a gun? It seemed he was stuck in
this house at least for a few days until his strength returned. Unfortunately, by then, the hot lead he'd been
pursuing would be stone cold.

"Do you need some help?" Wren asked, standing before him, the damp linens clutched in her hand. Her tea-
colored eyes shone with a purity that unsettled him.

He wanted to refuse her offer, to tell her he didn't
need any assistance, but that wasn't true. He was so
weak he could barely hold the washrag.

Keegan shook his head.

"Nonsense," she replied firmly. "You're as pale as
paste." She tossed the sheets on the floor and crossed
the room to his side.

Her very nearness swept him off guard. She smelled
great. Like delicate purple flowers and chicken soup.
Keegan had a sudden urge to bury his head against her
pert high breast and nuzzle there.

"Let me have it." She held out her palm for the rag
and helplessly, he handed it to her.

Damn, but he hated this! He was accustomed to issuing commands, not accepting them. Or at least he had been. In another life. Before tragedy struck.

"There's still blood in your hair." She clicked her tongue and dipped the washrag into the water. "This will probably hurt."

She pressed the cloth to the back of his head and Keegan hissed in his breath. It did hurt, but in a weird way it felt good. Wren's nimble fingers slipping through his hair and her chest was pressed so close to his mouth. If he leaned forward a mere fraction of an inch and stuck out his tongue, he could...

Stop it!

"Are you okay?" Wren hesitated and peered down at him.

He could tell from the owlish expression on her face that he'd frightened her somehow. Had he unconsciously jerked away from her? Had she heard his thoughts? That was a chilling concept. Keegan moistened his dry lips.

"Fine. I'm just a bit tired, that's all."

"Hang in there, I'll be done soon."

Carefully, Wren scrubbed his scalp until she'd removed all the blood. He had beautiful hair. Long, thick, silky. There was a large goose egg resting squarely on the back of his head, but the cut was small and shallow.

Her gaze traveled down his head to his neck, then lower to his right shoulder and upper back, her eyes taking in that scar. It covered an area the size of a hand towel. Her tummy twinged in response. They were deep burns. At least second-degree and in places, probably third. She longed to know what had happened, how he'd acquired the wounds, but she didn't dare ask.

The scars themselves told a sad story. He had endured a prolonged hospital stay and countless hours of physical therapy. He'd experienced a grave horror that had left him flawed and disfigured. Wren knew exactly what that felt like. To be hurting and alone. Empathy swarmed over her. She couldn't stop herself from feeling for this man.

At least a week's worth of beard growth ringed his angular jaw line and Wren caught herself wondering what he looked like with his face clean and smooth. He would appear younger, she thought, less disreputable.

"You need a shave," she said. "Do you feel up to it?"

He reached up a hand to stroke his chin. The resultant rasping sound was strangely erotic. Wren tried desperately to ignore the butterflies fluttering in her bloodstream. Was she out of her mind? Why on earth was she offering to shave him?

"It might make me feel better." Keegan nodded.

"I'll get fresh water."

Her hands trembled slightly as she carried the basin to the bathroom and exchanged cold water for warm. Peering into the mirror she noticed high color rode her cheekbones and her eyes shone impossibly bright. She seemed to be glowing. Like a woman in love.

Don't be ridiculous!

She shook the thought from her head, claimed one of her pink disposable razors from the cabinet and a canister of shaving cream off the shelf. She'd never shaved a man before, but how hard could it be? She'd been shaving her own legs since she was eleven years old.

But truthfully, it wasn't the task that troubled her, rather the effect of Keegan's proximity. She returned to the bedroom. He sat staring at her. Wren ducked her head and sucked in her breath, disconcerted and wishing she were anywhere but here.

She shook the aerosol can and sprayed a dollop of shaving cream into her palms. Rubbing her hands together, she then reached up to lather the gel onto his face.

His skin was rough beneath her fingers, his beard prickly. Keegan's eyes fluttered closed and Wren breathed a sigh of relief. It was easier to work without him staring at her.

After wiping the shaving cream from her fingers, she reached for the razor. She removed the plastic covering and stepped closer. She stood, razor poised, uncertain how to proceed.

He was such an impressive man, leaning back in the chair like a lion in repose, one arm cocked over the arm of the chair, only a thin blanket separating her from his naked body.

Gulping, she tentatively reached out and ran the razor down his cheek. She rinsed the razor in the basin, then returned to her project. She shaved each cheek, his jaw and chin, running the razor slowly over his skin. The tricky part was that little area between his nose and lips. She wondered if he might consider growing a moustache.

She reached out and carefully touched his nose. Using small movements she scraped the hairs away. The process was achingly intimate and she quickly became familiar with all the nuances of his face. The lines, the planes, the tiny wrinkles, the small blemishes. His cheekbones were high, his lips full. She should not be doing this. Such acts should be reserved for wives or nurses or barbers. Then again, she *was* his nurse. She didn't have to have a medical degree to provide him with creature comforts while he was ill. She was merely doing a job, that was all.

Her little finger lightly grazed his lip and she froze at the unintentional contact. Why was her heart beating so fast? Why did this wet, warm sensation flood her solar plexus? Why was she suddenly wondering what it would be like to have him kiss her?

Wren hurried to finish the task, flustered by her thoughts. Keegan seemed unperturbed, his eyes remained closed.

It was just as well he didn't find her attractive. Would he be flattered if he knew the direction of her thoughts? Or would he instead be repulsed by her? She was crippled, after all. Not many men considered a lame woman sexy.

Then again, he was burned. Perhaps he, unlike most people, could understand her. Perhaps life's tragedies had furnished him with the ability to see beyond physical appearances to the soul of the person beneath. Maybe he could see the real Wren Matthews and not the kooky spinster everyone else saw. Hope undulated in her chest, battering her rib cage with expectation.

Don't be fanciful. Even if that were true, Keegan doesn't know you well enough to judge you on your personality. And everybody knows where you rank on the looks scale even without the limp. You're definitely far below ten.

Blinking, Wren realized she'd been staring off into space, the razor clutched in her fingers. She looked down to see Keegan Winslow peering up at her.

Their gazes met, snared.

Her chest rose and she heard herself inhale sharply. She couldn't seem to tear her eyes away from him. The longer she looked, the more he drew her in with those magnetic black pupils. Like Alice in Wonderland, Wren felt as if she were tumbling headlong into a dark, endless vortex.

He never broke their connection.

Fear, sharper than anything she'd ever experienced, sprang into her throat. But it wasn't Keegan she feared, rather her own response to his heavy, virile expression.

''All done,'' she exclaimed. Turning, Wren fled from the room as fast as her aching hip would allow.

Chapter Five

He had to leave. His being here wasn't helping the woman. Wren's troubled brown eyes had told the story. She was scared of him, terrified even. The way she'd sped from the room in a panicked rush emphasized that fact. She had good reason to be afraid. He was a stranger invading her home, putting her innocent world in grave jeopardy.

Go.

Besides, he had his own agenda to pursue. Lingering in this warm, welcoming place would only soften him, and he had to be hard-edged and sharp-witted for what lay ahead. He could not allow himself to feel any emotion but retribution.

Time to vanish.

Where were his clothes? He surveyed the room from his vantage point opposite the bed. A large braided rug covered hardwood floors. An antique Tiffany lamp perched on the bedside table. A decoupage trash can rested next to a straight-backed chair.

Her place reminded him too much of his grandparents' small farm stashed away in the Wisconsin woods. That house had been cozy, homey, filled with laughter, hugs and spontaneous kisses. Until coming here, he hadn't thought about his grandparents' dairy in years. Keegan took a deep breath. The summers spent with Nana and Grandpa had been the best of his childhood.

But Keegan didn't want to remember. Fond memories served to heighten his sense of loss. He wanted to remain isolated, cut off from the things that made him human. Viewing the world with cold, unfeeling eyes was the only way to deal with the awful deprivation he'd suffered. Blinking, Keegan swallowed back the sadness flooding his mouth. Tenderness had no place in his life. Not now. Not ever again.

He spotted his jeans and shirt folded neatly across the back of the chair. His battered duffel bag rested in the seat with his hat and jacket draped across it. Keegan spied the toes of his boots protruding from beneath the lacy white bedskirt. Everything was present and accounted for, except the Magnum.

Hopefully, Wren would give him back his gun if he asked nicely on his way out the door. If she refused, he hated to think what he'd have to go through to acquire another one.

Running a hand across his clean-shaven face, Keegan recalled Wren's delicate touch as she'd gently tugged the razor over his skin. Why was he thinking about that? His mind should be firmly centered on his mission, not waxing romantic about Wren's fingers caressing his chin.

"Vacate the premises, Winslow," he growled to himself but his limbs felt sluggish and unresponsive. "Get up, walk across the room, put on your clothes and get out of here before Wren Matthews makes you consider things you have no business considering.''

Things like caring about another human being again? his mind questioned.

Yes. Exactly. That was why he had to leave. He could not afford to let himself feel anything for her beyond gratitude.

Placing both palms on the arms of the chair to brace himself, Keegan pushed upward. It took much more energy than he anticipated to rise to his feet. The blanket Wren had wrapped around him fell to the floor but he didn't possess the strength to pick it up.

His breath came hard. His head spun. He swayed.

Steady.

He reached out to grab the bedpost and exhaled heavily.

Dragging one foot in front of the other, he inched around the bed. It was only a few yards but it felt like miles.

You can do it. You've got to get out of here. You can't let Heller get away again. Not this time. Not when you're so close. The voice in the back of his head chided him, driving him onward.

He would rest, just for a moment, sit on the edge of the bed until his head quit spinning so viciously. Then he'd get dressed.

Turning his head, Keegan glanced outside. It had grown much darker in the short time he'd been up and he heard fresh sleet spitting against the window.

Damn.

A pain caught him low in the back, clenching his lungs in a viselike grip. A cough ripped through him and he winced against the hurt wrapping around his chest.

Come on, you wimp. Get up. Stop your bellyaching.

His old man's voice reverberated in his head. Leonard Winslow, career army, hard as nails and emotionless as they come. It had been difficult growing up with a drill sergeant for a father but it had made him tough.

Tough enough to withstand the horror of losing his wife and child. Tough enough to endure months of torturous physical therapy. Tough enough to stalk the thug responsible for his personal agony to the ends of the earth if necessary.

He had things to do. Places to be. A man to kill.

Bolstered, Keegan reached for his shirt. It was clean and smelled of soap. Wren. She'd washed and dried his things while he slept.

Guilt rippled through him. Wren Matthews didn't deserve to be exposed to the underbelly of life he brought with him. He was an angry man filled with the arrogance of retribution but he'd never considered revenge wrong. Justice, after all, had failed him. Taking matters into his own hands made sense. An eye for an eye. His father's way of thinking. When he thought about what Heller had done to his family, uncontrollable wrath surged through his system, supplying him with untold strength and determination.

What about forgiveness? his conscience needled him. *It's what Maggie would have wanted.*

Maggie, the pacificist. A kind gentle creature. They had been a mismatched pair, the serene earth mother and the army brat turned cop, but they'd balanced each other. She'd kept him on an even keel, anchored him with their daughter and he'd helped her to see the world wasn't always a rosy place. She had also urged him to remarry if anything ever happened to her, Keegan recalled with a grimace. And until Wren Matthews he'd found the thought of other women distasteful. Now, however, even though he was attracted to Wren, he couldn't entertain any notions of closeness. For her sake, if not his. He was too hell-bent on retaliation to be much use to any woman.

Yes, Maggie would forgive, as he suspected Wren Matthews would also forgive those who had trespassed against her. That lady wasn't any more suited for him than his wife had been. They were both too sweet, too caring, too compassionate to human suffering. But Keegan Winslow wasn't built that way.

What's done is done. Maggie and Katie are gone forever. Vengeance won't bring them back and might prevent you from finding future love. His conscience lingered, prodding him.

Maybe not, but it would go a long way in soothing the horrible anger that had been his closest companion for eighteen months.

And as for love, he didn't dare let himself feel *that* again. Whoever it was that said it was better to have loved and lost than never to have loved at all must not have had his family cruelly taken from him.

Forgive.

No! He almost shouted the word out loud. He could not, would not forgive. There was no clemency in his heart. Mercy was for the weak-willed. All he wanted was the satisfaction of staring into Connor Heller's face as the man begged for his life.

Keegan gritted his teeth and gave a dry sardonic smile at the image. Yes. He depended upon revenge and called it friend.

Tugging his shirt down over his head, Keegan sat back down on the bed, winded, listening to the air wheezing in and out of his lungs. He probably had pneumonia. Bronchitis at least, but he couldn't let illness deter him.

"Come on," he urged. "You can do it. Heller's here in Erath County, you know he's got family in the area. You've never been so close. Can't stop now."

In fact, all he needed was a map and a phone book. Gazing around the room, he noticed a plain black phone on the dresser, a phone book tucked underneath it. Crossing the floor, he retrieved the thin phone book and flipped it open to the H's. Jim Heller's name leapt out at him.

His finger shaking with anger and anticipation, Keegan traced the address. Farm Road 132, box 466. How far was that from Wren's place? he wondered. He didn't want to ask her for directions. The less she knew about him and his mission, the better. He'd just inquire after a map.

He pulled his jeans over his legs and wriggled into them. Pausing to rest again, he noticed it was almost pitch-black outside and the wind had picked up, whistling eerily through the trees.

So what? Get moving.

Leaning over, he ran a hand along the edge of the bed until his fingers collided with his boots. They'd been freshly polished, Keegan noted with a start.

Wren.

A strange sensation knotted his chest. He didn't like this, her taking care of him—polishing his shoes, washing his clothes, staving off his fever, shaving his beard. Leaving this haven was imperative before they both got hurt.

He clutched his boots in one hand and jerked his head up. A spasm shot down his neck. The room whirled. His knees telescoped and he pitched forward onto the floor.

Damn!

No matter how badly he might want to escape, Keegan had to face the truth. He was too weak and he was stuck here until he got his strength back. Stuck in close quarters with a big-hearted woman who didn't merit to come in contact with a blackguard like himself.

"Keegan?"

Wren rapped timidly on the door. In one hand, she carried a tray containing a steaming bowl of chicken noodle soup and a frothy mug of milk. If she wasn't so concerned about his health, she'd cut a wide circle around his room and leave him to his own devices, but in good conscience, she couldn't do that. Whether Keegan wanted to admit his weakness or not, the man needed her. She'd stayed as long in the barn as she dared, stretching out the evening milking and avoiding this moment. Wren cleared her throat and tried again.

"Are you okay?"

When she didn't receive an answer, alarm raised the hairs on the back of her neck.

"Mr. Winslow?" Wren twisted the knob and inched the door open. It creaked on its hinges. The room lay dark. She fumbled for the light switch on the wall and flicked it on.

She found him lying on the floor, fully clothed, staring at the ceiling. "Oh, my gosh!" she exclaimed, hurrying into the room and setting the tray on the bedside table. Had he fallen again? "What happened?"

"I'm all right." Keegan frowned, clearly irritated. He waved away her concern. "Don't fuss."

"Why are you out of bed? Why do you have your clothes on?" She crouched beside him, stuffing her hands deep into the pockets of her apron. Despite his gruff manner, Wren couldn't help herself. She had to know if he was oriented to time and place. That lick he took on the head might have serious consequences.

Wren gnawed her bottom lip. This was all her fault. She should never have left Keegan alone to get back in bed by himself. If only she hadn't experienced those bizarre sexual stirrings when she'd shaved him. She should have ignored those feelings, pushed them aside and stayed with him anyway, but she'd run, terrified of the emotions seething inside her whenever she touched this dangerous stranger. What was it about him that yanked so hard at her maternal instincts, and how did she go about defusing her reaction to him?

"What's your name?" she demanded.

"I know who I am." He sounded testy.

"So tell me."

He raised up on one elbow and rolled his eyes. "I'm Keegan Winslow."

"Where are you from?"

"The world. I'm an army brat."

"You're not being very helpful."

"What do you want from me?"

His aggravation hurt her feelings. She was just worried about him. Her lip trembled. "Fine. You're not accountable to me."

"I'm sorry," Keegan apologized. "I'm afraid I'm not a very good patient. I hate being helpless."

"That's okay." She blinked back the tears that had formed at the corner of her eyes. Why was she so sensitive?

"Chicago," he said.

"What?"

"I'm from Chicago."

"I guessed as much. From your accent."

"You'd make a good detective," he said.

Yeah. Right. He wouldn't think so if he learned of her inability to spot a con man.

"What day is it?" she asked, getting the conversation back on medical footing.

"Actually, I don't keep up with the calendar, but that has nothing to do with my head injury."

"It's the day before Christmas Eve," she informed him. "The twenty-third of December."

"Oh."

"So, why were you up?" She pulled her hands from her pockets and rested them on her hips.

"I wanted to get dressed but I then got dizzy. I thought it was safer to lie still on the floor."

Wren clicked her tongue and sighed. "Why on earth didn't you stay in bed?"

"I've got to be on my way."

"You're far too sick to be traveling in this weather."

"So I've realized." His tone was acrid, sarcastic.

"You've got a fever and probably a concussion from hitting your head," she chided.

"I can't hang around here. There are things I have to do."

"You, Mr. Winslow, are a very stubborn man." She looked down at him and their eyes linked. Wren gulped and wrenched her gaze away. What she saw in those dark depths sent shivers spiraling up her spine.

"So I've been told."

By whom? she wondered. His wife? Had that been a bone of contention between them, his pigheadedness? She wondered again if he was divorced or widowed.

"That soup smells good." He maneuvered himself into a sitting position and eyed the soup bowl.

"I'm glad to see you've got an appetite." She smiled, relieved that he seemed to be recovering.

Keegan didn't return her smile and Wren's quickly faded in response. She suddenly felt foolish.

"Here," she offered, reaching out her hand. "Let's get you back in bed."

He clasped her hand and let her pull him to his feet. She tried not to think about his strong, rough palm pressed flat against hers. She struggled to tamp down the complicated feelings fluttering in her stomach, warning her that she was treading on quicksand. She battled to deny that unnameable *something* that passed between them.

The man towered over her, tall and imposing. Keegan looked down. Wren peered upward, merely to check his stability but lost her clinical objectivity when she saw something hot and enticing glimmering in his eyes. His gaze lingered on her mouth and Wren feared what was going on in his head. Surely, he wasn't considering kissing her!

He leaned forward.

No. She couldn't handle this. Resolutely, Wren turned away before she discovered if he actually meant to kiss her or if she was just being fanciful.

"Here we go," she said with forced cheerfulness as she lifted the tray off the bedside table. "Have a seat."

Keegan obeyed, settling onto the bed. Okay. She'd been gripped by temporary insanity. Of course he hadn't meant to kiss her. She must have been nuts to think so. It scared her to believe she might have wanted the promise of his lips on hers.

Remember Blaine, remember Blaine, remember Blaine, she chanted to herself. *You were once so certain he was the man for you and look what happened.*

Goodness, what was she thinking? She wasn't seriously considering a relationship with Keegan Winslow! He was a drifter who'd be on his way as soon as the weather and his health allowed. She knew nothing about him. Still, she couldn't contradict the pull she felt in her solar plexus when she looked at him.

It's pity, Wren, that and nothing more. He's a sad, lonely case and he's managed to tug at your heartstrings. Don't get empathy mixed up with attraction.

"Thank you," Keegan said and reached for the tray.

Wren blinked as if jerked from a reverie. "Oh."

She looked as bewildered as he felt. For the briefest of seconds, Keegan had experienced a raging urge to kiss Wren, full and hard and long. For that moment in time, captured by the softness in her eyes he'd forgotten about his burn, about his suffering, about Maggie and Katie, about getting even with Connor Heller.

Feeling like a traitor, he stared at the bowl of soup which contained chunks of chicken, carrots, celery and onions mixed with thin egg noodles still steaming in a fat porcelain bowl. There was a mug of milk and a rose in a bud vase. Keegan pressed his lips together in a grim line. His Maggie used to add such homey touches to their meals. Candles and flowers, soft music and potpourri. Is that why he was so attracted to Wren Matthews? Because she reminded him of the woman he'd lost?

"What's this?" he asked, fingering the rose.

"It's not real. Just silk. I make them and I thought something bright might cheer you up."

He was so touched by her simple gesture that something warm and heavy pressed against the back of his eyelids. Keegan swallowed hard and turned his head away from Wren.

"If you don't mind," he said, purposely making his tone harsh. "I'd rather eat in private."

"Oh."

He heard the hurt in her voice but refused to look at her. He didn't want to encourage either her or the tender feelings swimming inside him. It had been a long day and he was weary beyond belief. He'd hit his head. That could explain his sudden emotionality.

"I'm not accustomed to being around people," he said, by way of explanation.

"Sure. I understand. I don't care for company either."

Head bowed, she limped from the room and Keegan felt as bad as if he'd kicked a stray dog. Dammit, why did he feel so sorry for this girl? She was none of his business and he had enough problems.

Could you have been a bigger rat? his conscience asked, but Keegan knew it was for her own good. He'd had the strangest sensation that she was falling for him, a man with murder on his mind.

"You were wrong, Wren. He didn't want to kiss you. The man doesn't even like you very much. But that's a good thing. Really." Wren talked to herself as she scrubbed the large soup pot.

An hour ago, she'd tiptoed back into Keegan's bedroom to retrieve his dishes. He'd been lying on the bed with his eyes closed, but Wren had the funniest feeling he was only pretending to be asleep. It was just as well. Perhaps the weather would moderate tomorrow and she could get out of the house and away from the distressingly masculine effects of Mr. Keegan Winslow.

The loaves of bread she'd baked for the teachers at school and her friends at church lay on the counter wrapped in red plastic wrap and topped with green bows.

It was kind of sad to think she might not be able to deliver the gifts she worked so hard to create, but even more unsettling was the thought she might be trapped home alone, throughout Christmas, with that dark silent man.

Wren glanced at the clock. Eight p.m. Drying her hands on a towel, she turned on the radio and crossed her fingers for good news. *Please let the sun come out tomorrow,* she prayed.

The last chords of "Silent Night," reverberated in the kitchen. She padded to the living room and added another log to the fire. Plopping down on the couch, Wren stared at the bedraggled Christmas tree. It looked like she felt, lonely, downhearted, confused. It cried out for something more. Twinkling lights, popcorn strands, construction paper chains, shimmering tinsel.

She threaded a hand through her hair and remembered those long-ago Christmases when Mother and Father were alive. When Aunt Tobie and Uncle Ray and her cousins, Lou, and Jean, and Karen lived close by. Before the car accident, before Uncle Ray's job had shipped him off to Saudi Arabia, before her cousins had grown up and gone about their own lives. Those had been such happy times.

There had been jokes and laughter and parties with lots of visitors. They'd gone caroling, drunk apple cider and hot chocolate. There had been a multitude of pies and cakes and cookies cooling on the sideboard. Jolly Uncle Ray had dressed up like Santa Claus, while spirited Aunt Tobie had played the part of Rudolph. Father had read *A Christmas Carol* aloud to all assembled and Mother had hung stockings from the chimney. They'd been so blissfully ignorant of their tragic future.

Wren bit down on her finger to keep from crying. Oh,

why had she brought that stupid tree home? Had she seriously believed a cedar tree could fill the empty space in her heart?

"Good news for all you folks dreaming of a white Christmas," the radio announcer's voice drifted into the living room. "That icy stuff will stay on the ground as temperatures remain stubbornly in the teens, but expect snow to join it sometime tomorrow evening. Yessiree, this is a once-in-a-lifetime occurrence for most Texans, so those of you with cabin fever, sit back, relax and enjoy the snow."

Wren groaned inwardly. Oh no. As a kid, she'd prayed for a white Christmas, to no avail. Now, when she least wanted one, the heavens had orchestrated it, to keep her stranded with Keegan Winslow.

Shaking her head, Wren crossed her arms over her chest. What was she going to do? She couldn't ask the man to leave. He was ill, the weather atrocious. Yet she was afraid to let him stay. Afraid of her own thoughts concerning the enigmatic stranger.

Well, if he was going to be here over Christmas, she needed a gift for him. But what? Wren bit her bottom lip, considering the problem. She could knit him a sweater.

In two days' time?

She could do it. If she started now and worked into the night. She wouldn't be able to sleep anyway, not with Keegan Winslow ensconced in the bedroom next to hers.

Why not? Christmas was about giving. This didn't have to be a sad, lonely time. At least this year she and Keegan would have each other.

Latent enthusiasm she'd long thought dead awakened in her belly. Yes. Getting to her feet, Wren hurried down the hall, eager to find her yarn and get started. Maybe she'd knit him a matching scarf, if she had time.

She passed his door, headed for her sewing room, when a sound drew her up short. Wren stopped and cocked her head.

What was that...?

It was an odd noise, soft and muffled. Wren stood very, very still, hardly daring to breathe as she listened for it again.

There it was. The sound of ragged breathing, of someone nearly crying.

The door was barely cracked. Wren crept forward and with the tip of her toe nudged the door inward. It swung open an inch or two and she peered into the darkness beyond.

She saw Keegan sitting on the edge of the bed, doubled over as if in pain. His head was cradled in his hands, his elbows resting on his knees, the image of despair. Wren's heart caught in her throat.

Could it be? That strong silent man weeping?

Shocked, Wren blinked back tears of her own. Tears born of sympathy. How many nights had she herself cried, alone, despondent, consumed with misery? But she hadn't expected tears from such a tough person. A man who lived life on the edge, hitchhiking from place to place. A man who carried a loaded gun and trusted no one.

She had thought him hardened by circumstances she could only guess at, had assumed he would be incapable of tears. She would have believed the shell around him was so solid, so unyielding that he'd be unable to release his emotions in such a discernible, demonstrative way. Wren would have expected Keegan to internalize everything, or even deny he possessed any feelings at all.

But here he was, sobbing his heart out like a lost little boy.

She ached for his sorrow. Wren backed away, silently easing the door closed behind her. Instinctively, she knew Keegan would be ashamed and humiliated if he realized she had witnessed his emotional breakdown.

Holding her breath, Wren slipped down the hall to her sewing room and, stunned, sat down at the sewing machine.

There was someone hurting worse than she. Someone who thirsted for the milk of human kindness but was afraid to reach out for it. Someone in such emotional pain it made her heart break.

She had to do something. She couldn't watch his suffering without trying to help. It was up to her to make this Christmas merry, to show him that all was not lost, that—no matter what had happened to him—life, did indeed, go on.

It was high time she stopped feeling sorry for herself and started reaching out to others. Perhaps that's what God had been trying to tell her when he deposited Keegan Winslow on her doorstep and sent a record-breaking ice storm to keep him there.

Resolutely, Wren lifted her chin and started to plan.

Chapter Six

"You don't have to try so hard," Keegan said. "I don't give a damn about Christmas."

"But I do!"

"You don't go to this much trouble when you're by yourself." He phrased it as a statement, not a question.

"No," Wren admitted cheerfully, "but this year I'm not alone. I've got company."

Keegan folded his arms across his chest, narrowed his eyes and watched her flit about the living room. What had come over the woman? She seemed possessed by the spirit of Noel. Gone was the quiet, shy lady he had first met two days earlier. She'd been replaced by a lively sprite who could pass for one of Santa's elves in those red leggings, green tunic and black boots. Dormant desire stirred. Disturbed by his gut reaction, Keegan glanced away.

A large cardboard box marked "X-mas stuff," lay open in the middle of the floor. Wren had draped a bright red garland around the mantel and hung mistletoe over the doorways. The scent of baked apples drifted in the air. Lights twinkled atop the Christmas tree, winking and blinking in the early-morning sunshine.

How long had she been awake? Keegan wondered. Since he'd slept, Wren had transformed the farmhouse into a winter wonderland. Candy-cane reindeer peered at him over lamp shades. A fat-bellied musical Santa perched on the coffee table, good-humoredly waving a gloved hand to the tune of "Santa Claus Is Coming to Town." Pinecone wreaths adorned the doors. She must have been at it for hours.

Uncomfortable with the lengths she'd gone to in order to impress him, Keegan stared out the window at the frosty ground.

"Are you hungry?" Wren asked. "I've made baked apples, sausages and oatmeal."

She wore jingle-bell earrings that tinkled gaily when she moved and the smile on her face metamorphosed her features into a beautiful work of art. How had he ever thought her plain? She practically glowed with an ethereal shine.

Keegan shrugged away the thought. He didn't want to admire her.

Wren chattered gaily about the weather, the season, the cows. Keegan kept quiet, refusing to encourage conversation. The more he talked to this woman the greater the risk he ran of getting involved with her. Better to keep his mouth shut and his defenses raised. He'd be leaving soon. Maybe today.

"You look much better this morning," she commented. "How do you feel?"

"Rested," Keegan admitted, tight-lipped.

Once he'd given in to the sorrow invading his heart last night and let himself cry, he'd fallen into a deep dreamless sleep. It was miraculous really, that he'd been able to drop his guard and surrender himself to slumber. He didn't know if that ability had been achieved through sheer exhaustion, or Wren's healing environment, or if his tears had in some way cleansed him. For the first time since that awful night he'd lost Maggie and Katie, Keegan had cried. Being here in this farmhouse that so reminded him of his grandparents' dairy farm, being with Wren, who reminded him so much of home, he'd experienced a spiritual catharsis that had been a long time coming.

But now, in the light of day, ashamed of the tears he'd shed, Keegan was ready once more to don his protective armor, to hide behind the mask of steely indifference that had served him so well for the past eighteen months. Tracking Heller required his full attention. He had nothing left over to give this woman. Not even a smile.

"Do you have a local map?" he asked abruptly, reminding himself he needed to locate Heller's father's farm.

"Just a minute." Wren went to the antique hutch in the corner and rummaged through the drawers. "Here's a Texas map."

"Do you have one of the immediate area?"

Frowning, Wren pursed her lips. "I should. Hang on."

She continued her search and eventually was rewarded. "Aha. This is it." She handed him a yellowed map.

"Thanks."

"No problem."

Wren led the way into the kitchen. Keegan followed, but stopped short and stared. The table was covered in a green-and-red felt tablecloth with a Nativity scene as a centerpiece. A Nativity scene identical to the one Maggie had set up every year. He laid a palm across his chest, felt his heart lurch jerkily.

"Sit down." Wren made shooing motions with her hands.

Uneasily averting his eyes from baby Jesus and the manger, Keegan pulled out a chair and sank down. The knot in his stomach tightened, his appetite suddenly vanished.

Wren buzzed around the kitchen humming to herself, then slid a plate in front of him.

"Aren't you eating?" he asked.

"I already ate."

Why did he feel a twinge of disappointment at the fact she wasn't going to sit beside him? Keegan picked up his fork and toyed with the baked apple, which was oozing cinnamon and butter. Not wanting to offend, he ate as much as he could.

He studied the map intently and discovered Wren's farm was located just off Farm Road 132. His gut squeezed. Nausea mingled with triumph. From what he could tell, he appeared to be a little less than two miles from where the senior Heller lived. Excited and nervous, he pocketed the map and pushed his breakfast aside. He needed to get outside, breathe some fresh air and formulate a plan.

"Have you done the milking?" he asked Wren.

"Not yet." Wren shook her head. "I was just on my way out."

"Let me do it," Keegan said, eager to escape the almost claustrophobic environment she had created with her decorating efforts. It was too much. Too relentlessly enthusiastic. Too overwhelmingly optimistic. Too damned much like Maggie's touch.

"Are you sure?" she insisted. "It was only yesterday you were running a high fever."

Why was she going to all this trouble for him? Her attention made him nervous. He preferred it when Wren had been frightened of him. He didn't want her to care, nor did he want to care about her.

She stood looking at him, a concerned expression on her face, her brown hair falling in wispy layers about her shoulders. He wished he'd stop noticing her delicate earlobes and her petite nose.

"I'm fine," he said gruffly, getting to his feet and pushing back his chair.

"Wait," Wren said. "Let me get my father's coat for you to wear. It's warmer than your leather jacket."

Keegan waited until she returned with a heavy overcoat and a pair of fleece-lined gloves. He shrugged into the coat, then worked his fingers into the gloves.

"There," she said, reaching up to brush lint from his shoulders.

He froze at her intimate gesture but Wren didn't seem to notice his reaction.

"Be careful," she cautioned. "The steps are still icy."

Nodding, Keegan moved away from her, fast. He did not want to dwell on the feelings her touch ignited inside him, nor acknowledge the fact that despite his best efforts to the contrary, this woman influenced him on a very basic level. His stay at this farmhouse was temporary. Very temporary. He could not encourage her in any way and he refused to be responsible for hurting her.

He made the mistake of looking at Wren one last time. She was staring at him, a sad expression on her pale oval face. Keegan tightened his jaw. Trust him to suck the joy right out of her holiday preparations.

Mumbling a halfhearted apology for not eating more breakfast, Keegan turned and walked from the kitchen, pulling the door closed tightly behind him. Funny, that wooden barrier proved far too thin for his taste. He wished for a much greater distance between himself and Wren Matthews. A span roughly the width of the Grand Canyon.

Wren scraped the remains of Keegan's breakfast into the trash and resisted the urge to cry. She pressed the back of her hand to her nose and inhaled sharply. Why on earth was she feeling so teary, so emotional? Just because he'd barely touched the food she'd worked so hard to prepare didn't mean it was a negative critique of her cooking skills. He simply wasn't hungry.

He didn't like my decorating efforts, either, she reminded herself. She'd stayed up all night, knitting his Christmas sweater, dragging the ornaments down from the attic and cooking him a hearty breakfast which he just picked over.

Her chest muscles burned. She had to stop being so sensitive. He wasn't rejecting her on a personal level. Besides, why should she care what Keegan Winslow thought of her?

Because I want to help him.

She realized that was true. For the longest time, she'd been wrapped up in her own problems. It had been easier to cloister herself, to withdraw from people and live like a hermit, than it was to overcome her setbacks and get on with her life.

If nothing else, Keegan Winslow had shown her it was time to lay aside her grief, and focus on someone else.

Sure, she'd suffered. She'd lost her parents, permanently injured her hip and been suckered by a charming con man. But enough was enough. She was twenty-nine years old. If she couldn't stop feeling sorry for herself now, when would she? The only way to overcome her fears was to let go and live in the present. She'd spent ten years wallowing in self-pity. The time had come to forget the past and embrace the future.

Wren plunged her hands into the soapy dishwater and peered out the window at the frozen ground, stunned by her revelation. A few hapless sparrows sat huddled on the telephone wires. Ice glazed the birdbath and the garden hose lay curled in frosty imprint on the dead grass.

Actually, once she'd decided to throw her heart and soul into the Christmas spirit, Wren's attitude had brightened. That surprised her. For so many years she'd gone through the motions of celebrating the season, and it had been a chore. But this year was different. From the moment she'd started on her project Wren felt lighter, freer, almost childlike.

It had been fun. More than fun. She'd grown excited, knowing she was making the holiday special for the cold, distant stranger who was in such dire need of Christmas cheer.

Keegan's reaction to her efforts, however, had been disappointing, but what had she expected? That he would suddenly drop his dour countenance and become jolly St. Nick? That he would honor her labor with a standing ovation? That he would care?

"Silly woman," she whispered under her breath.

Considering the way Keegan lived, unfettered and alone, Wren should have anticipated his response to her domestic scene. She'd gone overboard. She'd done too much, tried too hard. She couldn't force him to embrace Christmas.

Still, she wasn't going to give up trying. If anybody had ever needed a Christmas miracle, it was Keegan Winslow. She didn't know his story, couldn't name his pain, but that photograph she'd found and the burn scar traversing his back told the sorry tale.

Wren clasped her soapy palms together. She didn't exactly know what she was praying for but something inside her urged her to say the words.

"Dear Lord," she entreated. "Please bring Keegan out of the darkness and into the light."

The prayer seemed right, and fitting. It made her feel better. She wasn't sure what was happening to her but for the first time in many years, hope bloomed in her heart.

Hurrying down the steps, Keegan took in a fortifying breath. The cold air burned deep inside his lungs. Embracing the pain, he welcomed its frigid punishment. He had to remember who he was and what he was doing in rural Texas. Until Connor Heller was dead, or once more behind bars, he could not rest. He could not even enjoy the pleasure of Christmas Eve spent in the company of a fine, upstanding young woman. To allow himself that small luxury was a direct betrayal of Maggie. His wife's death must be avenged and unless he could accomplish that goal, Keegan could never have a life of his own.

The truly scary thing about Wren Matthews was that she made him yearn for hope. Until he'd met her, he thought all hope had died with his wife and daughter. To feel something begin to thaw in the apex of his heart heightened Keegan's apprehension.

"You've got to focus," he muttered, his breath chugging out in white puffs. "Think about Heller."

He knew the man was in the area. Had Heller come home for the holidays? Although Connor Heller and his brother, Victor, had been raised in south Chicago by their bookie mother, they had been born in Texas, and Connor's father still lived in Stephenville, not far from Wren's farm. It galled Keegan to think Heller was almost within touching distance. This was the closest he'd been to his quarry in the last six months, and yet there wasn't much he could do about it. Not now. Not yet. Not until the weather improved. Not until he recovered some of his strength. Keegan could only hope the storm was keeping Heller as icebound as he.

The man wouldn't be so stupid as to show up boldly on his father's doorstep, Keegan surmised. Heller was too crafty. He'd slipped through his pursuer's fingers several times over the last few months, and Keegan wasn't about to let it happen again. What he needed was a foolproof plan. Something to lure Heller out of hiding.

Shaking his head, Keegan pushed open the barn door and was struck immediately by the lack of warmth. Rather than mooing their discontent, the cows were lying down, burrowed in the hay.

The heaters had gone out.

Obviously, in her concern with taking care of him and decorating for Christmas, Wren had neglected to monitor the butane tank.

Keegan trod across the floor to twist off the main valve to the gas heaters, his gaze scanned the barn's rundown condition. The place sorely need renovating. The milking equipment was outmoded and the wooden stalls cried out for new braces. The roof leaked, as evidenced by the water stains marring the walls, and the fluorescent lighting, which flickered and buzzed, needed to be replaced. A couple of coats of paint wouldn't hurt anything either.

With only seventeen head of Holsteins, he doubted Wren even cleared a profit. It had to be tough, staying abreast of the constant demands. Keegan imagined the poor girl limping about the barn, trying her best to accomplish chores that were beyond her abilities.

She wasn't strong enough for this sort of work. She desperately needed help.

He wondered why Wren struggled to keep the dairy alive. From a financial standpoint it would make more sense to shut the place down than to pour money into restoring such a small endeavor. He shrugged. Perhaps the place was a tax write-off and nothing more. Still, it seemed like a lot of work for a simple tax break.

How did she even survive?

Perplexed, he ran a hand through his hair and accidentally grazed the bump on the back of his head. Keegan winced. He didn't have time to worry about Wren Matthews and her sad little life. His was no better. He would do for her what he could, then he'd get out of her way and go stake out Heller's farm.

He left the barn and circled around it, searching for the butane tank. He spotted two tanks a few yards away and breathed a relieved sigh. Thank goodness she had two. It wouldn't take much to switch the tanks and get the heat going again.

Keegan completed the task in a matter of minutes, then turned to go. When he did, he caught a glimpse of something disturbing at the edge of the woods bordering Wren's land.

Footprints in the ice. Fresh ones.

Fear rippled through him, raising the hairs on his arms. He moved closer to investigate.

The prints were large, made by at least a size-thirteen shoe.

Connor Heller wears a thirteen and a half, he thought. *Whoa, slow down, Winslow. Don't be jumping to irrational conclusions.* Still, the fact nagged at him.

He swiveled his head to the right and saw that the prints tracked across the backyard and down to the living room window.

Sometime in the night they'd had a Peeping Tom.

Anger shot through him at the thought of someone spying on Wren. But who? And why? He felt oddly jealous at the thought of someone watching her decorating the house while he'd slept.

Maybe Wren had an admirer. Someone too shy to speak to her. Or worse, someone who knew she was a vulnerable woman, living alone. It was a possibility.

Clenching his fists at the image his mind conjured of someone watching Wren, Keegan pivoted and followed the prints to where they disappeared into the woods. He'd damn well find out where they originated. It was the least he could do to ensure her safety.

Eyes to the ground, Keegan dodged tree limbs and skirted dead logs. At times, the prints were obscured in the mass of fallen leaves but he kept looking until he picked up the trail again.

He'd gone maybe a quarter of a mile when his lungs gave out on him. He had to stop to catch his breath and was then overcome by a coughing spasm.

Dammit! He hated being sick.

A few minutes later, he started off again, only this time to be betrayed by his legs. They quivered like jelly. He had to make a choice. Follow the footsteps or go back and help Wren with the milking. He didn't possess the strength for both.

You can't leave Wren alone, Winslow. The thought floated through his mind. *What if the voyeur returns and he's much more than a Peeping Tom?*

He recalled another time he'd left a woman alone when he shouldn't have. Keegan didn't have a choice.

Cursing under his breath, he retraced his steps until he reached the clearing where Wren's dairy stood.

He'd go tell Wren about the heaters being out and let the barn warm up in the meantime. Then he'd come back and start the milking. Keegan debated for a moment whether to tell her about the prowler or not. Finally he decided to keep quiet. At least for now. No point in alarming her unnecessarily.

Satisfied with that plan, he trekked to the house and knocked lightly on the door but didn't wait for an answer. He stepped inside. The kitchen was vacant and for a brief second, as he wondered about her whereabouts, anxiety gripped him. Where was she? But he heard her singing from the living room.

Wren was mutilating "Jingle Bells."

In spite of himself, Keegan smiled. Maggie hadn't been able to carry a tune in a basket either.

His smile completely disappeared. She *wasn't* Maggie! He had to remember that. There were similarities, yes. Both were kind, both maternal, sweet and good-natured. But where Maggie had been utterly dependent upon him, Wren blazed her own path, relying on no one despite the obstacles. Running a dairy, living alone, toting a gun to scare off an unexpected intruder. They might have been cut from the same pattern, but Wren was made of sturdier stuff.

The smile returned as he remembered Wren's fierce

stand when she'd threatened him with that inefficient little .22 rifle. At the thought of a firearm, he reached absently for the shoulder holster and .357 Magnum that wasn't there. Wren had also managed to disarm him. That said a lot about her courage.

Keegan walked to stand in the archway that connected the kitchen to the living room. Apparently Wren hadn't heard him come in over the noise of her own singing. She was perched on top of a stepladder placed strategically close to the Christmas tree, a white and gold angel clutched in her hand.

Crossing his arms over his chest, Keegan observed her.

She appeared like an angel herself, her fluffy brown hair layered about her face, her quiet smile radiating a pure, untouched glow. She wasn't the sort of woman men would whistle at on the street corner, but she did possess a forgiving quality that made a man dream of putting his head on those soft breasts and confiding his darkest secrets.

Stop it, Winslow. Stop this right now!

He shook his head. He could not, would not, confess anything to this woman. To even entertain the notion was ridiculous. He must bear his burden in silence. No one deserved to be sullied by his disreputable plans. Especially her.

Wren rose up on her tiptoes, struggling to affix the angel to the top of the tree.

Be careful, he mouthed wordlessly.

She must have caught a glimpse of him from her peripheral vision because she turned her head, smiled widely and lifted her hand in greeting. "Keegan!"

Genuine pleasure at seeing him beamed from her eyes.

She leaned forward, placing all of her weight on one corner of the thin, folding metal stepladder.

It wobbled.

Wren's mouth formed a startled circle. She dropped the angel. It fell to the ground and rolled under the tree. She tried to regain her balance but her hip twisted.

Keegan started across the floor, his hands out-stretched.

"Oh!" she squeaked.

The ladder wavered, then collapsed on its side. Wren's feet flew out from under her, her arms flailing in the air.

Keegan snagged her in the nick of time, and she tumbled heavily into his arms.

He stared down at her.

Wren peered up at him, her breath coming in quick shallow gasps.

His eyes widened as he drank in the sight of her.

She blinked and swallowed.

He clutched her close to his body, his forearm muscles bunching with the effort.

Her scent, a mind-scrambling combination of apples, cinnamon, lavender and vanilla, invaded Keegan's senses like cops converging on a crime scene.

Lips as tempting as rose petals in full bloom lay mere inches from Keegan's own. Her hair grazed his skin, her breasts nuzzled his chest, his arms cradled her bottom.

He hadn't expected holding her would affect him so strongly. He searched her face, startled by the sensations racing through his mind, his heart, his groin. She influenced him on every level, mentally, physically, emotionally. Even the first time he'd held Maggie in his arms Keegan had not experienced anything so intensely overwhelming.

Wren's eyes, wide and trusting, drank him in.

She shouldn't trust him. Not ever! Maggie had trusted him and look what had happened to her. He had nothing to offer Wren Matthews. Nothing to offer anyone but hatred, bitterness and revenge.

He must curb these bursts of desire he experienced whenever he was near this woman. She'd helped him in a time of need. He was grateful, and that was all.

And yet some part of him longed for things to be different, for him to be free to pursue her—but such a notion was laughable. He was chained. Leashed to the past and a commitment to bring the killer of his wife and child to justice.

Even if he could drop his obsession and stop chasing Heller, Keegan simply couldn't picture the two of them as a couple. Wren was fragile springtime; he was a winter's hard freeze. She radiated innocence; he reeked of sin and corruption. She personified the belief that people were basically good; Keegan knew the real truth.

No matter how mismatched they were, no matter how much he battled his growing awareness for her, he could not deny that she had awakened something inside him. Something raw, exposed and vulnerable. Something that scared him more than the thought of spending the rest of his life alone and wretched. He wanted to protect her as much as he had wanted to protect Maggie and Katie.

That realization, more than anything, corralled Keegan's desire. How could he possibly safeguard Wren when he hadn't even been able to save his own family?

Chapter Seven

"**Y**ou can put me down now," Wren whispered, her heart thudding faster than a hummingbird's wings. Her mouth was dry and her small hands trembled slightly as she pushed her bangs from her forehead.

Keegan was staring at her as if gazing at a far-off place. Where had he gone in his mind, she wondered. What was he thinking? Was he fighting an urge like the one swelling in her chest? An urge that ached to be sated with a long, slow, deep kiss?

A heated flush worked its way up her neck. She was foolish, fanciful, fickle. Just because she'd felt a quick, hot surge of desire when she'd landed in Keegan's masculine arms was no indication that he returned her feelings in kind.

"You shouldn't have been standing on that stepladder. It's too flimsy," he admonished, dispelling any idea that he had been thinking along the same lines as she. Then again, she shouldn't be surprised. She was crippled, after all, why would he want her?

Keegan put Wren on her feet and quickly moved away from her. "Why didn't you ask me to put the angel on the tree for you?"

"You were busy," she replied, hanging her head.

"You could have waited."

"I didn't think you wanted to be involved with the Christmas preparations."

He put his hands on his hips and glared at her. "I told you I didn't give a damn about celebrating Christmas, but I'd prefer it if you didn't break your neck in the process."

His dark hair flopped across his forehead. Shadows filtering in through the curtains accentuated his high cheekbones. A thrill fluttered through Wren and she placed a hand on her stomach. It was absurd and irrational, her response to this man. But heaven help her, she couldn't do anything to change her feelings. Call it magic, chemistry or good old-fashioned lust, she could not disavow the fact that this stranger, this odd mystery man, this loner with a chip on his shoulder, stirred her blood with a fierceness she'd never before encountered.

"I'm sorry," she apologized.

He bent over to pick up the angel from the floor and dusted bits of tinsel from her skirt. Without using the stepladder, he reached up and settled the cherub on the top of the tree.

"Is that where you wanted it?" His voice had softened somewhat, but he did not return her smile.

"Yes." Wren nodded. "Thank you."

He stepped back. "I've got to go back and milk the cows. There was a problem."

"Problem?" Wren pursed her lips.

"The heaters were out in the barn. The butane tank was empty but I switched it over to the second tank."

"Oh, dear," she sighed. "I've been meaning to order more butane, but I don't get my paycheck until after the holidays. It's tough being a teacher and getting paid just once a month, especially at Christmastime."

"You're a teacher?"

Wren smiled. "High-school English."

Keegan made a face. "My worst subject. I preferred math."

She realized, happily, this was the first piece of personal information he'd offered her. "I'm pretty miserable at math, I'm afraid. Do you use math in your job?" she asked, attempting to engage him in conversation about himself.

His jaw clenched and she wished she hadn't probed. She hated it when strangers quizzed her. She should have kept her mouth shut and let him reveal himself to her at his own pace. Now she'd ruined the small bond she'd established.

"I'm no longer employed," he said curtly.

Wren bit her tongue to keep from asking him why. Did she really want to know if he was involved in something illegal? "I'll help you with the milking," she said. "Let me get dressed."

She donned her coat and they went outside together. It didn't seem as cold as it had the day before. The wind had quieted and they could hear the restless cattle mooing loudly from the barn.

Keegan had made a rapid recovery, Wren noted. He stayed one step ahead of her, as if reluctant to walk beside her. Could she blame him? With her limp, she slowed him down. He also kept shooting furtive glances at the trees. She wondered why.

They entered the barn and chaos greeted their eyes.

A water pipe running along the top of the barn had

burst. Water spewed over the cows in a powerful stream and ran ankle-deep across the floor. It mixed with straw and cow manure. Bossie angrily butted her head against the stall door; wood splinters flying in her wake. Wren stood openmouthed, not knowing what to do.

"Where's the cut-off valve?" Keegan asked, shouting above the deafening din.

Wren turned. Water caught her full in the face and sent her sprawling to the floor.

In an instant, Keegan was there, pulling Wren to her feet. "Are you okay?" Awkwardly, he brushed the seat of her pants.

She nodded, shivering more from his touch than the cold water soaking her skin.

"The valve?" he repeated.

"We can reach it from the loft."

He took her hand and led her gingerly around the disgorging pipes. Even though they both wore gloves, Wren savored the feeling of her hand in his.

"Pipe probably broke last night when the heat went off," he said, making his way over to the stairs. "Once I got the heat turned back on and the barn warmed up, the pipes defrosted."

He started up the stairs. Wren couldn't help but note his confident walk and the way he filled out his jeans.

Stop thinking like that! she chided herself.

"What a mess," she said, shaking her head to clear her mind of erotic thoughts.

"Don't worry, I'll help you clean it up." He glanced down at her and Wren's heart tripped. No matter how she might try to fight it, she couldn't seem to stem the riotous emotions he created inside her with a mere glimpse of those smoldering dark eyes.

"I'm so glad you're here," she said. "This would be a nightmare without you."

He reached the loft, turned and offered his hand to help her up. "How do you manage alone?"

"Not very well, I'm afraid. Until six weeks ago one of my students used to work for me after school, but he broke his leg playing football and I've been in a bit of a pickle ever since."

Keegan let go of her hand and went over to investigate the layout of the plumbing. Wren watched him move with long, graceful steps. A stab of envy knifed through her. Since the accident, she hadn't possessed the freedom to walk so unconsciously aware of her movements.

He quickly shut off the valve. "Come on," he said.

They returned to the barn below, which had quieted considerably, although the cows were wet, cold and thoroughly miserable. Wren clicked her tongue. Hours of work lay before them.

Keegan looked at Wren. Wren looked at Keegan.

"Merry Christmas," he said, then grinned.

His smile was worth it, Wren thought. The burst pipe, the soggy cows, the mucky barn floor. Just seeing his lips curl up at the corners warmed her insides like a bowl of hot stew.

She started to giggle.

"You think this is funny?"

She nodded and slapped a hand over her mouth.

"You've got a warped sense of humor, Ms. Matthews, you know that?" His eyes actually twinkled. Wren caught her breath, mesmerized. He looked like the man she'd seen in that photograph—warm, welcoming, full of love and laughter.

His gaze caught her and he hesitated, as if realizing he'd slipped and let down his guard. Immediately, his features sobered. "Where do you keep your tools?" he said.

"The shed. I'll show you."

Darn! What had she done to break the spell, to chase away the moment? Wren mulled this over while they tracked down the tools and set about repairing the pipe. How could she replicate that smile? She ached to see it again. For that brief moment, Keegan Winslow had forgotten about the demons chewing his soul.

What were those demons? she pondered, holding the equipment for him while he repaired the damaged plumbing. They must be very powerful to keep him so imprisoned.

Wren watched his shoulder muscles bunch as he reached above their heads to remove the piece of split pipe. She thought of the wound hidden beneath his layers of clothing and pursed her lips. She suppressed a sudden desire to brush her mouth against his scarred skin and kiss away the hurt and pain buried there.

"Do you have a welding torch?" he asked.

"Huh?" Wren blinked.

"You need a new piece of pipe, but I'll see if I can weld it together long enough to hold until we can get to the plumbing supply store."

"Yes." She nodded. "I do have a welding torch somewhere."

She found the torch and a mask. Keegan stayed outside to weld while Wren began the cleanup. Taking old feed sacks from a shelf, she started wiping the cows dry.

Keegan returned to patch the pipe and then helped her complete the chores. He had to stop to rest several times. Wren noticed his breathing became labored with little exertion and that worried her, but she said nothing. It wasn't her place to tell him what to do but oh! how she ached to wrap her arms around him and nestle him protectively against her breasts.

"How big was your grandparents' dairy?" Wren asked, during one rest period.

"They kept a hundred and fifty head. Jerseys mostly."

"I like Jerseys," Wren said. "They're not as stubborn as Holsteins." She indicated Bossie with a wave of her hand.

"I think Holsteins are smarter, though." Keegan perched on a hay bale. "And then there's the ongoing argument about milk production."

Wren nodded. "Tell me about it."

"How often is your milk pickup?"

"My dairy's so small the truck just comes once a week. On Tuesdays." Wren smiled. It was nice to have a normal conversation about something they both shared an interest in.

"May I ask a personal question?" Keegan asked, and looked her in the eyes.

Wren curled her toes inside her boots at his gaze and told herself to calm down. "Sure."

"Why do you bother with the dairy? It's obvious you're losing money."

"It's been in my family for three generations."

"Oh."

"What happened to your grandparents' place? Does it still belong to your family?"

Keegan shook his head. "No." He sounded wistful. "My father was an only child and he hated the dairy. After my grandfather died, he sold the place."

"I can't imagine giving my place up. It's such a part of me and my roots. It's hard work but I can't imagine not doing it."

"Sometimes I wonder what would have happened if

I'd been old enough to buy the dairy from my father.'' Keegan stared off into space as if peering into the past. ''How different my life might have been.''

Regret colored his face. Wren reached out to touch his arm but he quickly moved away.

''Time to get back to work,'' he said, shattering the tentative closeness they'd forged.

He had a hard time accepting sympathy. As someone with a physical disability, she could understand. Still, that understanding didn't blunt the sting of his rejection.

They went back to work and four hours later, exhausted, they had completed the cleanup. Oddly enough, Wren felt darned good in spite of her achy hip. She remembered the days when her mother and father had worked the dairy, side by side. They'd toiled with a minimum of conversation but a maximum of closeness. True partners, functioning together like a cog and wheel. She and Keegan made that kind of team. Focused, determined, they got the work accomplished.

They stripped off their outer clothes in the foyer, hanging their coats on pegs and leaving their boots to dry on newspaper spread in the entryway. Wren pulled off her gloves, then ran her fingers through her mussed hair, knowing she must look frightful.

''Thank you,'' she said.

''Don't mention it. It's the least I could do to repay you for your hospitality.''

''Mr. Winslow.'' She hesitated.

''Yes?''

''I've got something to ask you.''

He raised an eyebrow.

Wren spoke in a rush, wanting to spill the question before she lost her nerve. ''I know you said you were just traveling through, but you also said you didn't have a job.''

Keegan waited silently.

She was shy. This was hard for her. She might be making a grave mistake, especially if he took her up on her offer. ''If you've been considering remaining in Stephenville for a while, I want you to know that you've always got a place to stay.''

His dark eyes glowed. Her stomach plummeted. Oh no, had he misread her intentions? Did he think she was proposing something more than employment?

''I mean,'' she said desperately, knotting her fingers together. ''If you want to stop hitchhiking, if you've thought about staying put...'' Lord, she was making a mess of this.

''Just say what's on your mind, Wren.'' Keegan's tone was surprisingly gentle.

She cleared her throat, moistened her tongue. ''Mr. Winslow,'' she said. ''Would you like a job?''

She was trembling. Why? Was offering him a job such a monumental step for her that it resulted in tremors? He knew she was a shy woman. Taking the risk of asking a stranger to become her live-in farmhand couldn't be easy for her.

Keegan appraised Wren. Was she afraid he was going to say no, or yes?

Her chin quivered. She clasped her hands together in front of her. Her eyes were wide, her face pale. She needed help running her dairy, that much was clear, but he wasn't the man for the job.

He shrugged.

''You don't have to give me an answer right away,'' she said, rushing to fill the silence that was lengthening.

It was tough saying no to that sweet face.

"Just think about it."

"All right," he said, knowing there was no way he could stay. Still, some part of him yearned to say yes. It would be a welcome relief to let go of the hunt, forget his vendetta, take up residence at this dairy and remain here until he had time to heal, but he did not enjoy that luxury.

"We could fix up the loft," she suggested. "And make it more habitable."

She twisted the hem of her shirt around one finger. The gesture reminded him of Katie. His daughter used to wind her finger around her hair when she was nervous. Nostalgia knifed his gut. What would it hurt to humor Wren, to tell her he'd be happy to take the job? She would find someone else when he was gone and he wouldn't have to reject her now, wouldn't have to see the disappointment in her innocent brown eyes.

"I can't pay much," she said. "Room and board is about the best I can offer."

Hell, he was getting soft. When, in the course of the last eighteen months, had he let another person's wants or needs get in his way? With Maggie and Katie gone, no one else had mattered.

Until now.

That realization stunned him.

He cared about Wren Matthews. Not in a romantic way, he quickly pointed out to himself, but as a person.

And that was a fatal mistake.

Only brute, killer instinct had kept him alive this long. Only hatred and anger had assured his survival.

What would the guys at the station house say if they could see him now? Would they be proud of his dedication to hunting down Heller? Would they be appalled at how far he had sunk, letting malice consume his soul? Or as cops in an unjust world, would they praise his vigilantism, applaud his determination?

After Keegan had recovered from his burns, his best friend, Bill Rizer, had begged him to come back to the police department. For a time, he had considered it, even though his job had been the catalyst that had destroyed his family. If he hadn't shot Victor Heller in self-defense during a drug bust gone bad, then Connor Heller would not have targeted him.

An eye for an eye.

Something unpleasant slithered through Keegan's veins. Guilt? Remorse?

The cops had arrested Connor while Keegan was still in the burn unit and the trial had been swift. Keegan had gone in a wheelchair and swathed in bandages. He wasn't about to miss seeing the killer get his due. Heller been given a life sentence. See, Keegan's friends had pointed out, trying to be supportive and encouraging, the legal system does work.

And then Connor Heller had escaped from Joliet Prison. He hit a guard over the head, took his clothes and simply walked out the front gates. After that there had been no choice, no question of going back to the force.

No matter what the outcome, Keegan could never be a cop again. He couldn't go back to patrolling a beat, watching as victim after victim fell prey to vultures like the Heller brothers.

Keegan's hand formed a fist and sweat beaded his upper lip. Truth was, he hadn't given one minute's thought to what would happen to him after his show-down with Heller.

"What are you running from?" Wren Matthew's

husky whisper broke through his thoughts, bringing Keegan sharply back to the present.

He stared at her. Her eyes were bright, her face sincere. She shifted uncomfortably from his hard-edged assessment but did not look away. She was a brave woman. No one could deny that.

"I'm not running from anything," he said flatly.

"Then why don't you stay here? Stop moving long enough to review your life, see what went wrong."

Oh, he knew what had gone wrong. Knew far too well. Long nights on the open road had given him plenty of opportunity to think. He should have been in the house that night with Maggie and Katie. He should have saved them, or died with them. Instead, he'd been working overtime, more concerned with his job than with his family.

Keegan gritted his teeth. The old rage boiled inside him, fresh and new. For the last three days he'd let himself be lulled by Wren Matthews's sweetness. He'd foolishly allowed her kindness to soothe him. Had he forgotten so quickly? He had to avenge his wife and daughter, had to redeem his mistakes. There was no other way to live with himself. Dammit, Maggie and Katie were dead because he had let them down!

Keegan's breath shot out in ragged spurts. He frowned deeply as he fought the urge to break something with his bare hands. He scanned the kitchen.

Fear leapt to Wren's face. Her color paled. She took a step backward. "Keegan?"

He growled, unable to answer her.

"Did I say something wrong? Did I do something wrong?"

Keegan shook his head. He was scaring her. She deserved better from him. Calm down. Bottle the rage. Save it for Heller.

"Nothing," he mumbled. "I was thinking about the past."

Tentatively, she reached out and touched his shoulder. "It must have been awful."

"Worse."

"Tell me about it."

"No." He tensed and she quickly drew back.

"As you wish."

"Don't be upset with me, Wren. It's got nothing to do with you."

Wren forced herself not to shudder. At this moment, Keegan appeared as dark and ominous as he had that first night on her porch steps. She'd been out of her mind to think she could help a man with emotional problems that obviously ran so deep. Trying to soothe Keegan Winslow was like trying to make a pet of a wild lion. Her misguided mission had been doomed to failure from the start.

Turmoil dogged him. Relentlessly. Tension tightened the lines in his face, anger vibrated from his pores. She could hear guilt hidden in the undertones of his voice.

She reached out to touch him but he jerked away and whirled around to face her, his eyes menacing. Her heart thudded at the force of his rage. "You need to talk to someone, Keegan, and not keep your feelings bottled up."

He shook his finger in her face. Wren was taken aback by his vehemence.

"Don't dare tell me what I need. You're not my wife. Got it? Don't ever think you are."

Chapter Eight

Wren raised a hand to her neck. "I never...I didn't mean..." Tears crowded her throat and to her horror, slipped down her cheeks. She didn't want him to see her cry, to know she was so weak. "What happened?" she whispered. "Back there in the barn you were so nice, so helpful. What did I do wrong?"

"You've made a mistake. I'm not a nice guy."

"I don't believe that," she said, blinking away her tears.

"You're kidding yourself."

His words were ugly but the pain in his eyes was real. He was like an orphaned boy who'd been shuffled from foster home to foster home, never putting down roots, never making loving ties, never trusting anyone. He was filled with rage at the world and all the people in it. She'd witnessed such aggression in some of her troubled high-school students. Adverse life circumstances caused those kids to construct a tough outer exterior. Rather than withdrawing, they tended to go on the offensive. Just like Keegan was doing right now.

He lashed out because he was hurting. Wren understood this, but understanding him and helping him come to grips with his past were two different things. She wasn't a trained psychologist. If she was smart, she would pack up his things, send him on his way, get him out of her life forever. Yet for some reason, she simply could not give up on him. The same way she refused to give up on her most unfortunate students. She had to try.

"There's a decent man hiding behind your angry bravado," Wren accused. She might be shy, but she was not a coward. Her limp might have made her self-conscious, but that didn't mean she was a pushover. When it came to something important, Wren Matthews stood her ground. "I see flashes of him."

"Oh, yeah? How can you be so sure?"

"There's an intense internal struggle going on inside you. It's easy to see."

He rolled his eyes. "You're romanticizing me."

"I have a feeling about you." She said, placing a fist over her stomach. "A gut reaction."

"Really? Are you such a great judge of character that you always rely on your instincts? Have you never trusted the wrong man, Wren Matthews?" His glare was colder than the ice outside keeping them bound together.

Wren sucked in her breath as she thought of Blaine Thomas. Yes, she'd once trusted the wrong man. She'd been so lonely without her parents that she had wanted to believe in Blaine's love. But with Blaine, she had dismissed her instincts. Her gut feeling had told her he was too nice, too accommodating, too willing to center his life around hers, but in desperation, she'd brushed aside her reservations, and she'd paid a high price for ignoring her intuition.

And now, the same instinct that had warned her off Blaine was driving her forward to Keegan.

"Obviously, something is making you behave this way. Something terrible that's happened in your past. You don't want to tell me and that's fine. But this is my house and it's Christmas Eve, and I won't have you bullying me."

"I'm sorry," he said. "You didn't deserve that."

"Apology accepted. Now, why don't you take a warm bath and try to relax?"

He turned without a word and headed for the bathroom, stunned by the thoughts running through his head.

Wren's composure amazed him. Most women would have run from him. Maggie certainly would have. His wife had hated confrontations. That had been one of the biggest conflicts in their marriage. She'd never stood up to him. Never voiced her opinion. He'd secretly disliked that aspect of her personality. Keegan, a cop by nature, thrived on conflict. Not that he had wanted constant discord in his home. Not by any means. He'd had his fill of that growing up with a drill-sergeant father, but he might have preferred a little more spice in his marriage. Some fire, a dose of passion. In Wren's company he experienced that hot spark that had been missing in his relationship with his wife.

Maggie had always been sweet and accommodating, acquiescing to his every desire. Her innocence had attracted his protective nature, but if he was honest wouldn't he admit that her clinging dependence had sometimes been a strain? He always had to be in control, never letting down his guard or allowing his true feelings to show.

Wren's steadfast refusal to bow to his ire had calmed Keegan. She had brought him back to the present and demanded accountability for his actions. Like a cool breeze on a scorching sunburn, her unwavering conviction soothed him.

She was quite a woman. Soft and sweet like Maggie, but at her core existed a rod of steel that commanded Keegan's respect. His admiration for her grew. That first night, when he knocked on her door, he would never have suspected she was such a strong and capable person.

Keegan closed the bathroom door and peered at his reflection in the mirror. His eyes appeared haunted, his face gaunt with shadows. Threads of gray flecked his hair and the wrinkles on his forehead deepened when he frowned. When had he started looking so old? He was only thirty-five, but felt three times that age. The last eighteen months had exacted an exorbitant toll.

Did Wren Matthews find him attractive? he wondered. Or was he just a charity case in her eyes? This morning, when he'd captured her in his arms after the ladder toppled over, he hadn't imagined that expression of desire written on her face, had he?

His affinity for her bothered him. There was no place in his life for her. Even if he wasn't chasing Connor Heller, which he was, his heart lay dark and empty. He had nothing to give, nothing to offer a special woman like Wren.

For one fleeting moment, when she'd offered him the job as her dairy hand, he had been sorely tempted to accept. He didn't have to pursue Heller. He could leave it to the police, start his life afresh, here and now in Stephenville, Texas. He had the choice to release his rage, and allow Wren's caring concern to heal him.

Stripping off his shirt before the mirror, Keegan turned halfway and stared at his back. The burn scar was an ugly red gash across his skin, a grim reminder of all he'd suffered. Heller had done this to him. Marked him for life. He couldn't forgive and he must not forget.

While Keegan showered in the front bathroom, Wren got undressed in the back. The explosion with Keegan had rattled her more than she cared to admit. She'd stood up to him, but at what cost? She dropped her bathrobe to the floor and stepped into the warm bubble bath.

The pipes groaned as water came on in the other bathroom.

Wren tried not to envision Keegan standing naked under the rough spray, but she couldn't halt the picture that rose in her mind.

She saw his palms spread out against the tile, his head lowered under the shower spray as he allowed the water to sluice down his ravaged back. She thought of his burn and pressed her fingertips to her mouth. Closing her eyes, she let her mind travel over his body, boldly exploring him in her imagination the way she would never dare do in real life.

His torso was long and lean, like a long-distance runner. His chest honed like a washboard, his buttocks firm and tight. Wren sucked in her breath, felt her insides grow warm and soft.

Oh, heavens! Never in her wildest fantasies had she been so attracted to anyone.

She should be afraid of him, but instead his edginess drew her. He was more seductive to her than twilight shadows were to fireflies. He promised the dangerous excitement of unharnessed electricity. Making love with this man would soar beyond anything she had ever experienced.

Making love?

Heaven forgive her, how long had she been thinking about making love to Keegan Winslow? Back there in the kitchen, when he'd challenged her, his aura as explosive as nitroglycerin, she'd experienced a strange burning in her groin and a tightening of her senses. Suddenly everything had seemed much more intense. His masculine scent dominated her nose, the sight of his lips incited a hungry desire to be kissed, the sound of his clipped speech sent shivers skyrocketing up her spine. But she had ignored the sensations, denying them because she didn't want to hazard a guess at what such feelings might signify.

She wanted this man. As she'd never wanted another. And she could not have him.

Something drove him; he was on a mission she did not comprehend. A sense of purpose was all about him, desperate and grave. He seemed to be punishing himself for something. Hitchhiking, living on the road, running from kindness, shunning concern. He carried monstrous guilt on his shoulders. What had he done? she wondered. Who had he wronged and why?

"If he would just talk to me," she whispered, then realized how that sounded. Why would he spill his soul to her? She was nothing to him. Ironic really, a few days ago she'd been wishing for a silent dairy hand and now that she'd gotten him, she wanted nothing more than for Keegan to talk, to fill her ears with tales of his sorrows.

"Forget it, Wren. Treat him tenderly, show him kindness while he is here and then let him go."

Wren sank down in the bubbles. Sound advice. But could she follow it?

* * *

She was at it again.

Humming cheerfully, cooking relentlessly, giving him those warm soft smiles. Keegan had finished the second round of milking chores only to come inside the house and find two brightly wrapped packages under the Christmas tree.

Oh hell, he thought, *please don't let those packages be for me.*

The very notion that she'd prepared him a gift sent Keegan into panic. He had nothing to give in return. He'd stopped thinking about other people a long time ago. It had never occurred to him that Wren might give him a present.

"Have a seat in the living room," she called from the kitchen. "We'll take our supper in front of the tree."

Keegan groaned inwardly. Wren was determined to make this a real Christmas, in spite of his reluctance.

"Do you need any help?" he asked, feeling rather restless and unsure of himself.

"Nope."

Stuffing his hands in the back pockets of his jeans, Keegan prowled the living room. A bookcase lined the wall opposite the fireplace. He stepped closer, and began to peruse the titles.

Dickens, Twain, Hemingway. Steinbeck, Cather, Poe. All the classics bound in leather. What else did he expect? She was a high-school English teacher.

It seemed eons ago that he had been in high school and read these books. Once he'd actually been young and eager to leave home. If he'd known then what he knew now, Keegan would not have been in such a hurry to escape his upbringing and rush headlong into the future.

"The TV trays are in the hall closet," Wren said,

coming to stand in the archway. She wore a festive apron with Santa Clauses embroidered on the front. "Would you mind setting them up, please?"

Keegan shrugged and headed for the closet. He tried to remain as silent as possible. If he said nothing at all it might be easier to keep from blurting out his feelings to her. Although he didn't want to talk about his past, Wren was making it harder and harder to stay quiet. He longed to explain his behavior to her, to let her know that his outrage at the world had nothing to do with her. But he simply could not allow himself to reveal his inner feelings to this woman and involve her in his sordid affairs.

He set up the TV trays, then picked up the remote control and switched on the television to the six o'clock news.

"Hey, boys and girls," the newscaster exclaimed. "We've just received news that Santa Claus has been spotted in north Texas."

Nostalgia reached out and slapped Keegan. Hard. The memories hurt. Instant gooseflesh carpeted his skin. He pressed his lips together against the emotion as he remembered the last Christmas he'd spent with Maggie and Katie.

His daughter had been three at the time, just old enough to really enjoy the Santa Claus myth. She'd been so wound up on Christmas Eve, hopping and jumping in perpetual motion, chattering nonstop, her blue eyes wide and expressive. He could still see her sweet smile and her blond hair, so much like her mother's, billowing around her little face. It was the last time he remembered being happy.

The television announcers kept yakking about Christmas and Santa Claus and reindeer but the noise sounded very far away. Keegan felt as if he were moving down a long dark tunnel, headed straight into a bottomless pit. Hands trembling, he reached out, hit the remote control and clicked off the television.

Perspiration covered his brow and he was breathless. Had the fever come back?

"Keegan?"

He glanced up to see Wren staring down at him.

"Are you all right?"

"Yeah."

She gave him a worried frown. "Do you mind if I listen to the weather?"

He shook his head.

"You're sure you're okay?"

Keegan turned the television back on without answering.

"Folks, this is going to be a Christmas for the record books," the weatherman said gleefully. "Temperatures are warming up to around twenty-five degrees and we're expecting a blanket of snow measuring two to three inches for tomorrow morning. Yes, you heard right. For the first time since 1934 we're going to have a white Christmas in north central Texas."

Wren clapped her hands and squealed as excitedly as Katie might have done. "A white Christmas. Isn't that wonderful?"

Keegan shrugged. He was from Chicago. A white Christmas was no big deal.

"This is so great," Wren enthused.

Her eyes twinkled merrily as St. Nick's himself, her lips curled into a smile prettier than a Yule wreath. The color in her cheeks was rosy and he realized with a start that she'd applied makeup. She seemed different from when he'd first met her. Happier, somehow.

"I'm glad you're here to share this Christmas with me," she said. She sounded so positive of her statement. Did she mean it? Was she truly glad to have his company?

"You're pretty hard up, Wren Matthews, if you're grateful for the company of a scoundrel like me."

"You're too rough on yourself."

"You don't even know me," he accused. "For all you know I could be a murderer on the run from justice."

That was true. It might have been Connor Heller who had shown up on her doorstep instead of him. In fact, it might actually be Heller lurking in her woods. That gave him pause. In her naiveté would she have welcomed the killer as readily as she had welcomed him? Fear traipsed invisible footprints over his skin as he thought about what could have happened to her.

She gave him a pitying look. "I don't know what's happened to you, Keegan Winslow, but at some point you've got to start putting your life back together."

He didn't answer.

The oven timer dinged, punctuating his silence.

"Dinner's ready," she said and left the room. "Come and get your plate."

He followed her into the kitchen and waited while she dished up their meal. Roast Cornish game hen, cornbread stuffing, green bean casserole, hot buttered rolls. The food brought memories of other holidays, happier times. Keegan accepted his plate from her with murmured thanks and headed back to the living room.

"Christmas Eve was the only time Mama let us eat in the living room," Wren said, positioning herself in the chair next to him. "We'd sit and eat and look at the tree."

Keegan studied his plate. He did not want to know

how Wren Matthews had spent her past Christmas Eves. He did not want to get involved with her on a personal level. Couldn't she see that? Didn't she know it was for her own good?

He ate while she chattered. She seemed compelled to fill the silence. Concentrating on the delicious food, Keegan tried not to think. Not about Christmas, nor Maggie and Katie, nor his inexplicable connection to Wren.

Suddenly, she stopped talking.

Emptiness echoed, disturbed only by the faint sound of wood crackling in the fireplace.

He put down his fork and looked over at her.

Tears shimmered in her brown eyes.

"What's wrong?" he asked, alarmed.

"Do you find me repulsive?" Wren asked, batting away tears with the back of her hand.

"God, no!" Keegan declared. In fact, the opposite was true. He found her devastatingly attractive. Those wide limpid brown eyes could be his undoing if he dared let her get close enough.

"Then why do you always look away from me? Like I'm a freak."

"Wren," he protested.

"You don't have to be ashamed of your feelings. If you're repelled, then you're repelled."

"I'm not put off by your disability, dammit. Not one bit."

"What is it about me, then?"

"It's not you. I've been alone a long time," he admitted awkwardly, abashed to think his behavior had made her doubt herself. "I'm not used to being around people. Really, it's me. My social skills are the pits."

"You're sure it's not my limp?"

"Honey," he spoke softly. "Your limp doesn't detract from your loveliness one whit."

Her cheeks pinked. "You don't have to lie. I know I'm not lovely." She folded her hands in her lap and glanced down at them.

"Says who?"

She shrugged. "Experience."

"Well then, you've been having the wrong experiences."

What directed him to do what he did next, Keegan couldn't say. He simply knew he had to do something to make her feel better. He put his TV tray aside, moved over to her chair, crouched before her and cupped her chin in his palm.

"You possess an inner beauty, Wren, something that can't be faked or manufactured with makeup and clothing. Don't let anyone ever tell you otherwise."

"But my limp..." She crumpled her napkin in her fists. He could tell this was a touchy subject with her. What cruel fools had made fun of her?

Keegan shook his head. "It's only a handicap if you let it become one. Actually, I think it makes you more attractive."

"You do?" Her eyes sparkled at his words.

"Yes. Your limp tells the world you've suffered through something traumatic and survived with a good attitude intact."

"Not every man would agree with you."

"If a man thinks less of you because of your physical imperfection, then he's not much of a man and certainly not worthy of your time and consideration."

"Thank you," Wren said, "for saying so."

He patted her lightly on the knee and rose to his feet. The gesture caused her heart to soar. Keegan had admitted it. He found her attractive! Now if she could get him to talk about himself, to trust her with his story, perhaps they could work past the barriers between them and build a real friendship. The idea pleased her.

"Would you like to know why I limp?" Wren asked.

"Only if you want to tell me." He returned to his chair and leaned forward. Elbows resting on his knees, he gave her his undivided attention.

Wren took a deep breath to steady her nerves then launched into her history.

Keegan listened. Truly listened. His eyes never left her face and he didn't once interrupt. Wren had merely meant to tell him about the accident where their car spun out on ice and slammed into a guardrail killing her parents, but he was so encouraging, nodding his head and murmuring his sympathy, that she found herself telling him her most shameful secret—giving Blaine Thomas money for some crazy scheme to make the dairy successful.

When she'd finished almost an hour later, Wren took a deep breath and settled back against the chair.

"I'm sorry to hear about your parents and what you went through," Keegan said.

"Thanks."

"As far as that creep that took your money, don't feel embarrassed. It happens to a lot of people. You were just too trusting."

Wren gave a harsh laugh. "I know. I let the whole thing get to me. I haven't even dated since then. After Blaine, I've been afraid to trust men."

Their eyes met. Something in Keegan's look caused her to exhale sharply.

"Until you," she said.

"You shouldn't trust me either, Wren. It's not wise."

"Do you mean me harm, Keegan Winslow?" Goose bumps popped up on her arms, but she never dropped her gaze.

"You don't know anything about me."

"So tell me about you."

He shook his head.

"Why not?"

"You're better off not knowing."

"Have you done something bad?" she asked. His statement should have scared her but it didn't. In fact, his mysterious behavior heightened her interest. An insatiable passion to learn more about him had Wren squirming on the edge of her chair.

"I do not have honorable intentions," he said.

"Toward me?"

"Toward anything."

His blunt scowl caused her muscles to tighten. "Why? Because of that burn?"

"You don't really want to know. It's a long, dark story."

Wren pressed her lips together. "All right. I can respect your right to privacy."

"Thank you."

She got up from her chair, her pulse sliding rapidly though her veins, and cleared the dishes from their television trays. She couldn't name the emotion surging through her. Was it fear, dread, temptation, desire? Perhaps a bizarre combination of all four.

What had he done that was so terrible? Why was he on the run? Keegan Winslow was a complete paradox. One moment he was kind, tender, reassuring her that she was an attractive woman despite her limp. The next second he would turn cryptic, warning away her questions with his moodiness and his refusal to communicate any information about his personal life.

She didn't know what to make of him, but she was determined this was going to be a pleasant Christmas Eve, no matter what. Leaving the dishes to soak in the sink, she made her way back to the living room.

"It was the tradition in my family to open gifts on Christmas Eve," she said. "What about you?"

"We always unwrapped ours at dawn at Christmas morning," Keegan replied.

Wren limped over to the tree, picked up the two gaily wrapped packages beneath it and brought them over to Keegan. "These are for you." She stretched out her hand.

"You shouldn't have."

She shrugged. "It's Christmas. I couldn't let it pass without doing something."

"I...I don't have anything to give you," he said.

"Yes, you do."

"What's that?"

"A smile."

His lips lifted lightly at the corners.

"I want a real smile," she said.

"It's tough for me."

"I know."

He tried again. This time the smile spread to his eyes. Wren smiled back, felt her face warm.

His grin widened in response to hers.

"There! That's so much better. Now open your presents."

Keegan fumbled with the tape. His dark hair curled down the collar of his turtleneck sweater, almost obliterating any evidence of his burn scar. Wren thought he was the handsomest man she'd ever seen. Especially when he smiled.

Keegan tore through the wrapping paper and opened the box. He lifted out the gray-and-white sweater she'd spent the whole of last night knitting for him.

"It's beautiful," he exclaimed. "But how—where did you get it? You haven't been out to shop. You don't know my size—"

Was it her imagination or did he stumble over the sentiment?

Silently she lifted up her knitting bag, showing him the gray and white yarn.

"You did this yourself?" He raised the sweater to his face, brushed the soft material against his cheek. There was awe in his voice that touched and pleased her.

She nodded.

He blinked and looked away. "Thank you."

"The other present is a matching scarf," she said, feeling nervous. "I thought you might need something warm when you're hitchhiking on the road. I'd hate for you to get sick again."

"That's very thoughtful of you, Wren."

"Hey, isn't that what Christmas is all about?"

"You deserve a gift from me. Something more than a smile, but I have nothing to give."

"That's so wrong."

"What do you mean?"

"You fixed my water pipes. That was a wonderful gift. Do you have any idea what it would have cost me to have that done?"

"I owe you much more."

"If you really feel that way, then stay and help me work the dairy."

Something dark swept across his eyes. "I can't. I wish I could, Wren, but I can't."

"What can I say to change your mind? I need your help, Keegan. Badly."

"You'll find someone else."

"I suppose you're right."

But she didn't want anybody else! She wanted Keegan Winslow. Ached for him, actually. She couldn't sleep at night because he dominated her brain. She had trouble eating because her stomach was all jittery in his presence. Her knees went weak when he smiled and when he touched her, she melted. Already the thought of him leaving had created a gaping hole in her heart. After having his solid, comforting presence around for the last few days it was going to be even harder returning to her solitary existence.

He stood in the archway between the kitchen in the living room, a sprig of mistletoe dangling above his head. His tall physique filled the room, his broad hands were laced together in front of him. He drew her more powerfully than any magnet and with more force than a runaway freight train.

Impulsively, without any thought to her action, Wren crossed the floor to stand beside him. This could be the last chance she had to taste those lips and she'd be a fool to pass up the opportunity.

Keegan looked down at her, obviously unaware he was standing under the mistletoe. Wren reached up and placed a hand on each shoulder.

"I've got something else for you," she said. "Shut your eyes."

He obeyed, letting his eyes fall closed.

Her hands trembled but she didn't care. She'd been longing to do this since he'd caught her when she tumbled off the step ladder. Pursing her lips, Wren rose on tiptoes and pressed her mouth to his.

At first, Keegan did not react.

She lifted her arms, threaded her fingers through his hair and gently tugged his head down. Just when she started to feel like an oversexed female making unwanted advances, Keegan groaned low in his throat and accepted the challenge.

His mouth covered hers, hard and hungry.

Wren held on tight, savoring the moment, knowing she might never again taste anything so wonderful.

Keegan's strong arms pulled her flush against his body.

Welcoming him like a long-lost lover, Wren opened her mouth, anxious to increase their intimacy. Despite her doubts, despite what was good and smart and rational, her instincts urged her to deepen the kiss, to consume this man.

His tongue dipped past hers and she felt as if she'd swallowed heaven. Sensations quite unlike anything she'd ever experienced exploded inside her. Heat and sweet. Tangy and tart. His kiss was far more incredible than her fantasies.

Keegan moaned as she pressed herself intimately against him, unsure exactly of her own intentions, simply knowing that she wanted more from this man. His mouth left hers, trailing hot kisses behind her ear.

''Wren…oh sweet little Wren…'' He sighed into her hair.

His hands moved up and down her back, at first softly, then gradually with more pressure. She rolled back her head, allowing his mouth tender access to her exposed throat. She gasped as one of his hands moved from her back, around her ribs, just below her breasts.

It had been so long since Wren had felt wanted and desired. It was so good to be held in masculine arms, to feel the beat of his heart mirroring the frantic pace of her own pulse. Somewhere in the back of her mind she knew that the pleasure was not in being held in any masculine arms, but in Keegan Winslow's. When Blaine had kissed her it had all been lies, but with Keegan it felt so real, so right.

But was it the real thing? her subconscious nudged. Hadn't Blaine tricked her, at least for a while? How could she be sure she wasn't fooling herself with Keegan, too?

He'd warned her about himself. Had told her emphatically that he couldn't be trusted and yet she was stubbornly denying his words, seeking to prove her instincts correct.

Or was it more? Was she ignoring the facts, purposely blinding herself to his faults, intentionally creating excuses for his life-style simply because she was starting to fall in love with him?

In that instant, Wren knew it was true. Somehow, in some way, over the course of the last three days she'd managed to lose her heart to this man. An unusual man, and one she knew absolutely nothing about.

Chapter Nine

Keegan disentangled her arms from around his neck and set her firmly on the ground. "I know you're attracted to me, Wren, but your affections are misguided."

"Misguided?" she repeated.

"I can't return your interest."

Wren gave a nervous laugh. "I don't know what you mean, Keegan. I don't expect anything from you. Nothing at all. You were just standing under the mistletoe." She gestured at the green sprig sporting white berries dangling over their heads.

Who did she think she was fooling? Certainly not him. That kiss had been special and potent as dynamite. And if he weren't involved in tracking down Connor Heller, if he weren't so angry and embittered, if revenge didn't dominate his very soul, he might have allowed himself to wonder where that kiss could have led.

"Just a friendly Christmas kiss?" he asked.

"Surely you didn't think it was anything more than

that?'' Her bottom lip trembled, belying her breezy denial.

''No.'' He shook his head but inside he felt hot and shivery. ''Of course not.''

Wren forced a smile but Keegan could tell tears hovered below the surface. He hadn't meant to lead her on, to hurt her. This wasn't supposed to happen. He'd purposely kept himself isolated for the last six months, avoiding people, living within himself, concentrating on his mission to the exclusion of everything else. He had no right to encourage her interest in him, even though his own interest had kept growing stronger.

If only the storm hadn't hit. If only he hadn't gotten sick and prolonged his stay. If only he hadn't stumbled upon Wren Matthews's dairy in the first place. One thing was perfectly clear. He had to get out of here, and fast. Before anything further happened between them. Because next time, he might not be so satisfied with a kiss.

''Thank you again, Wren, for the sweater and the scarf. It was a very thoughtful.''

''You're welcome.''

''I'm feeling tired,'' he said awkwardly. ''I haven't really recouped from that fever.''

She nodded.

''Think I'll hit the sack early tonight.'' He stretched his arms over his head and faked a yawn.

''Sure.''

''Good night, then.''

''Good night.''

Keegan headed for the bedroom, guilt weighting his conscience. He stopped in the hall, and turned back to gaze at Wren.

She looked like an angel against the starry backdrop

of the twinkling Christmas tree lights. A lump rose in his throat but he swallowed it down.

"I'll be leaving first thing in the morning."

She said nothing to dissuade him, and for that Keegan was grateful.

"Could I have my Magnum back? Please."

She hesitated a moment then said, "All right."

Retrieving a key from the rack mounted on the wall near the telephone, Wren opened the cabinet and withdrew his gun. She walked over to him and pressed the weapon into his hand.

"Good luck, Keegan Winslow," she whispered. "I hope you find what you're looking for."

Wren picked up the telephone receiver. It was still as dead as it had been on the night Keegan arrived. Apparently, the severe storm and the holiday had kept the phone company from repairing the line as quickly as they might otherwise have done. She sighed. If the phone had been working, she would have called her fellow teacher, Mary Beth Armand, just to hear a friendly voice.

Perhaps it was a good thing. Did she really want to tell Mary Beth what a fool she'd been, and risk having that gossip spread about the school yard?

Wren sat in the rocking chair by the fireplace, gently rocking back and forth, her fingertips lightly caressing her lips. Why on earth had she kissed Keegan Winslow and what had she expected it to solve? Had she really believed she could get through to this man? What did she want from him?

A shoulder to lean on.

That thought floated through her mind. It had been so

long since she'd experienced love, since she'd had someone to depend on.

But wasn't it more? The urges roiling through her
lower abdomen suggested her needs went much deeper
than a simple shoulder to lean against.

Sighing, Wren got up and went to the kitchen to wash
the supper dishes. To cheer her glum spirits, she turned
on the radio before starting her work. ''Joy to the
World'' played. In an effort to fight the sadness growing
within her, Wren began to sing along.

She'd learned something important from her associa-
tion with Keegan Winslow. Although he wasn't hers to
keep, his appearance in her life had taught her a valuable
lesson. She had been living in the shadows for too long,
hiding from life, avoiding people and using her injury
as an excuse not to trust.

And then Wren had met someone with fears and needs
greater than her own. A man who carried a heavy burden. A man too fearful to let anyone under his skin and
into his heart, no matter how badly he needed human
contact.

Without meaning to, Keegan Winslow had raised a
mirror to her soul and allowed her to peer into her destiny. If she stayed on her current path, reclusive and shy,
she would end up just like him. Bitter and alone, with
no one to care for her. In time, like Keegan, she would
come to accept that fate. Perhaps even to prefer it.

Thank heavens he had turned up on her doorstep.
He'd brought her an important message. Get involved
with life. Start caring about people. Think of something
besides your own sorrow.

In the course of caring for him, Wren's whole outlook
had been altered and she approved of the changes within
herself. It was past time to start loving again. Probably

not Keegan Winslow, but someone. She was eternally grateful to him for the unknowing gift he'd bestowed upon her this Christmas.

"Now for the ten o'clock news," the radio announcer's voice cut in as the last chords of the song ended.

Wren dragged the dishrag across a plate and half-heartedly listened to the broadcast. She knew the deejay would be talking about Santa. She didn't need any reminders that this was the holiday season and she had no friends, no family, no children or husband to spend it with.

"We have some rather unpleasant news to report this Christmas Eve," the announcer said.

What happened, Wren wondered rather sarcastically, Santa have a sleigh wreck?

"A report has come in that an escaped felon has been spotted in the Stephenville area."

Wren cocked her head. *What?*

"The man, one Connor Heller from Chicago, Illinois, was seen three days ago hitchhiking in rural central Texas."

Wren's blood froze.

"Heller escaped from Joliet Prison last June. Despite an all-out manhunt, the convict has eluded capture for the past six months. Heller was in prison for setting fire to the home of a prominent Chicago police officer, whose wife and young daughter were killed in the blaze. Heller set the fire as an act of revenge against the officer, who shot Heller's brother in the course of an undercover drug sting."

No! Wren shouted internally as trepidation snaked around her stomach and squeezed hard. She recalled her initial terror that night three days before, when she'd found Keegan Winslow standing on her back porch. She'd been afraid of him then.

"In order not to alarm the public, police did not release information about Heller until his appearance in the area was confirmed. However, officials are now urging extreme caution if this man is encountered. Heller, thirty-five, is approximately six-one and weighs two hundred and ten pounds."

Heller was from Chicago. So was Keegan.

Wren paced, her bad leg thumping clumsily against the floor.

Heller was thirty-five. Keegan was about the same age.

She balled her hands into fists, sucked air into her lungs in thick, ragged gulps.

Heller was six foot one. Keegan was, too.

But the voice in the back of her mind disagreed with the conclusion she was close to drawing. Keegan wasn't anywhere near two hundred and ten pounds.

"He could have lost weight," she spoke out loud. "He's been sick, on the road. It wouldn't be hard to drop twenty-five pounds."

"Connor Heller has one distinguishing mark," the announcer continued as if witness to Wren's internal debate. "He suffered burns on his neck and back as consequences of the fire he set."

The news punched her square in the gut. Pain shot through her abdomen. Wren sank to her knees as she considered the horrible evidence she'd just heard.

"No," she whimpered. "It can't be." But no matter how she might long to deny the facts, Wren couldn't ignore the truth staring her in the face. Keegan Winslow was really Connor Heller, and she'd stupidly given him back his .357 Magnum.

* * *

Keegan lay on the bed, listening to the radio whisper Christmas music. He had a lot of thinking to do. About Maggie and Katie, about Connor Heller, about Wren.

Wren Matthews.

His body trembled at the thought of her and that kiss. She'd kissed him so boldly, so bravely, as if by pressing her lips to his she had the power to change both their wretched lives.

He admired her courage. Applauded her determination. But he could not embrace her efforts to comfort him, no matter how much he might long to find oblivion in her welcoming arms.

Still, her scent lingered on his skin. Sweet as springtime and twice as nice.

After Maggie's death, he'd sworn there would never be another woman in his life. How could he have a moment's peace as long as the scar on his back served as a vivid reminder of all he had lost? How could he hope again when his heart had been ripped from his chest and scorched to cinders? How could he take a risk on love when he was incapable of feeling anything but rage and revenge and hatred?

Yet what was this softening sensation he experienced deep inside his chest whenever he thought about Wren?

No! He could not, would not, let himself feel anything for her. Keegan hardened his heart and told himself lies.

Wren Matthews was nothing but a scared little schoolteacher. Crippled and clumsy, naive and foolish. So foolish in fact, she'd given him back his Magnum. She trusted him.

He grunted out loud. In her naiveté it was a wonder she'd survived this long. He reached his hand under the pillow and curled his fingers around the gun. The dead weight of it calmed his fingers. Yes. That's what he needed to remember. The satisfying vengeance hard steel could bring. He refused to think about tender kisses, warm embraces and the smell of home-baked cookies.

But his conscience refused to be dammed up any longer. For six months he'd managed to keep his doubts and guilt concerning his mission at bay, but no longer. He didn't have to do this. He could allow the police to bring Heller in. He could simply stop the chase. He could drop his anger, lay down his weapon and welcome love into his life once more.

Love brings pain, his dark side reminded him. *Lots and lots of pain.* If he dared love again then he was risking loss again.

Keegan shuddered. He could not live through another experience like the one that robbed him of his wife and child.

Wren isn't Maggie, something in the back of his mind persisted. *She's stronger, tougher, a survivor.*

Closing his eyes, Keegan fought against the memory that flared in his brain. In a hissing blue burst, he was back there. Eighteen months ago. At the scene of the fire. He clenched his fists and groaned, his whole body rigid as his mind was consumed with the flashback.

Four a.m. He'd just gotten off duty after a wild double shift. It was still dark. He had walked home because he'd left the car for Maggie to use, the station house only a mile and a half from their home.

Keegan caught a whiff of something and crinkled his nose. Smoke. He remembered frowning and wondering who had a fire in their fireplace so late in the season.

Then he saw the flames licking high above the neighborhood rooftops and he sobered quickly. He started to run, praying that the fear building inside him was a lie. It wasn't his house, his home, it simply couldn't be.

But it was.

He recalled the wail of fire trucks, the bright orange blaze. The firemen had held him back from rushing into the house.

He twisted in agony at the memory but he couldn't shut it out. He was there again, breathing in the filthy air, feeling the heat, tasting the acrid burn.

Nothing could have restrained him at that point. He jerked free of the fireman pinning him to the ground and threw himself into the inferno screaming Maggie's name.

He'd fought the smoke and the flames to find her. She was in their bed, curled into a ball, her head under the pillow.

"Maggie," he'd sobbed her name.

His wife hadn't even tried to run, to shield their daughter. She'd simply given up. He hadn't been there to guide her and Maggie had not known what to do without his leadership, so she'd done nothing.

Keegan had gathered his wife into arms, then turned to leave with her cradled to his chest, wood burning and crackling all around them. His grief had been so great he hadn't heard the movement behind him.

In the blinking of an eye, he found himself sprawled on the floor. A shadowy figure sprinted from the room. Connor Heller.

The roof had collapsed then. His shirt had caught fire, burning his neck, shoulders and back. The firemen had pulled him from the wreckage, although he had tried to fight them, howling that he wanted to die.

But he'd lived.

Keegan bit down on the inside of his cheek. Hard. That suffering was the reason he could not encourage Wren, nor stay one day longer at her dairy. The respite had served its purpose. He had no business thinking of Wren Matthews, her kiss and what it really meant. He didn't deserve her. He was a horrible protector, an awful husband. It was his due that he must spend the rest of his days in loneliness and regret.

You're damned lucky to have the opportunity to grab a second chance with such a woman as Wren, his conscience argued with him. *Stop feeling sorry for yourself.*

Second chance! Who was he kidding? There was no such thing as a second chance for a man like him.

It's Christmas, the voice continued. *A time for miracles.*

Except he didn't believe in miracles, not any more. Keegan shifted restlessly on the bed, reached over and clicked on the bedside radio.

''Now for the ten o'clock news.''

Groaning, Keegan got to his feet. The last thing he wanted to hear was report of another Santa Claus sighting, but the announcer's next words stopped him cold before he could switch off the radio dial.

Connor Heller had been seen in the area. His blood ran cold while at the same time he smiled to himself in the darkness.

Jubilation combined with grim relief. Yes! As of three days ago, Heller was still here, probably trapped like himself by the ice and cold. Keegan had planned on waiting until morning before leaving Wren's hospitality and going to stake out Heller's father's place, but this latest turn of events convinced him he needed to depart right away. It was now or never. The road he'd been traveling for so long was finally at its end. Determined, Keegan pulled on his boots and strapped the Magnum to his chest.

He had to hurry. Sooner or later Heller would hear

the report and get out of Stephenville as quickly as possible. Keegan couldn't afford to lose him. Not again.

The sound of glass breaking in the other room drew his attention. Keegan cocked his head and listened. *What the hell?*

"Wren?" He pushed open the door and stepped out into the hallway. "Are you all right?"

He saw her standing in front of the gun cabinet, shattered glass around her feet.

"Hands up!" Wren said, raising the shotgun to her shoulder and peering down the barrel. She aimed at his heart, a grim expression on her face. She wore an ankle-length flannel nightgown and fuzzy pink slippers. The sight was so incongruous, he almost laughed.

"What's going on?" he asked.

"Why don't you tell me, Mr. Heller?" Her hands trembled but the tone of her voice was pure granite.

Heller? Wren had obviously heard the news report and assumed *he* was Connor Heller.

"Wait a minute, Wren, I can explain."

"I don't want to hear any more lies!"

"Will you just listen?"

"Why? To give you time to wrestle this gun away from me? Don't stand so close, back up against the wall."

Keegan did as she asked. "I'm not Connor Heller. I really am Keegan Winslow. Heller murdered my family."

She hesitated. He could tell she wanted to believe him but she was afraid and he couldn't blame her.

"Put down the shotgun, Wren and let's talk."

"Show me some ID. Prove you're Keegan Winslow."

Keegan sighed. "I quit the police force after the fire and turned in my badge."

"A driver's license then."

Hell, he'd had his wallet stolen back in Nebraska. "I don't have any ID on me, but I swear to you I'm not Connor Heller."

"You expect me to believe that?"

"Come on, Wren, do you think you might actually be attracted to a murderer? You've got more sense than that."

"I've been fooled before. Blaine Thomas was a con man and I didn't realize it until it was too late."

He saw the pain in her eyes as she warred with herself. "What about that kiss?" he whispered. "Don't tell me that wasn't special because I know it was."

"The radio said Heller has a burn scar on his back," she insisted, stubbornly raising her chin and ignoring his claim that their kiss had meant something. "Since you can't prove you're not him, then that burn stands as proof you are."

"Heller was burned in the fire he started. The fire that killed my wife and daughter. That same fire scarred me too."

"Not good enough." She didn't even blink. "I think you are Connor Heller and you're just pretending to be Keegan Winslow."

"Wren." Keegan sighed his exasperation. "If I were Connor Heller and intent on hurting you, then wouldn't I have done so by now?"

"I don't know," she admitted. "You needed my help. I was useful to you."

Time was of the essence. He had to get back on Heller's trail as soon as possible. He couldn't stand here all night debating the issue of his identity with Wren.

"Fine. Believe what you want. I'm leaving." Keegan made a move for the door.

"Don't." Her tone was firm, deadly.

"Look." He lifted his palms. "I've been tracking Heller ever since he escaped from prison. I finally narrowed down my search to the Stephenville area. Heller's father lives just a few miles from here. If we heard that newscast then we can be sure Heller will hear it, too. I've got to find him before he takes off again."

"Good try," she said, "but it doesn't impress me. You and I are going to get in my truck and drive into town where we're going to see Sheriff Langley. If you really are Keegan Winslow, then you can prove it to him."

"That'll take hours, driving in the ice, and that's if we don't end up dead in the ditch on the way."

"So? If you are who you say you are it won't matter. And if we die then we'll both be out of our misery, won't we?"

He winced at the thoughtlessness of his words. Her parents had died as a result of wrecking on the ice and Wren had suffered a lifelong injury. The fact she'd be willing to chance venturing out in the weather told him exactly how determined she was.

"I can't give Heller time to get out of town."

"That's a chance you'll have to take."

"No," Keegan replied. "I'm not going with you." He turned on his heels and headed for the door.

She pumped the shotgun.

The noise echoed loud and ugly in the room.

"Don't make me use this."

"Wren," he said, without even looking at her. Instead, he rested his hand on the doorknob. "If you want to stop me, then you'll just have to shoot me."

Sweat pellets formed on her brow. Was he telling the truth? Was he really Keegan Winslow or could he be that cold-blooded murderer, Connor Heller?

"Please," she begged, "step away from the door."

What would she do if he refused to obey her command? Could she bring herself to pull the trigger? She was confused, upset, angry with both herself and the man in front of her.

His eyes narrowed. He tugged the brim of his fedora down lower over his forehead, zipped up his leather jacket and scowled.

"I'm leaving now."

He opened the door and the cold night air ripped through the room, sending a frigid chill chasing up her nightgown and snow flurries whirling into the foyer.

Once more, he glanced at her over his shoulder, his dark eyes smoldering. "I never meant to hurt you," he said. "No matter what happens I want you to believe that."

Wren gulped as her emotions rioted. Could she honestly have fallen in love with a murderer? Her heart thudded to her feet. She had a history of falling for inappropriate men. A man had taken advantage of her good nature. A man had used her. Could she have made another terrible mistake? Could her instincts have truly been so wrong about him? Or had she been blind to all the signals—his aloof moodiness, his reluctance to talk about himself, his insistence that he was no good for her. He'd warned her and she'd been too stupid to pay attention.

"Goodbye, Wren Matthews," he said, giving her a little salute. "You deserve the best in life and I hope you find a good man to love you."

The shotgun lay heavy in her hands. Her throat was dry, her muscles tense. Keegan wore the scarf she'd knitted him. How could she shoot a man wearing the scarf she'd made him? Besides, what if he was Keegan Winslow and not Connor Heller? She had no alternative but to allow his escape.

He disappeared into the night, enveloped by darkness and snow. Wren felt the loss straight to her soul.

Keegan was gone.

She crossed the room and shut the door. Empty. Her life was empty once more.

He simply could not be Connor Heller. If he was, how could she be feeling such tender things for the man?

Then again, at one point in her life, she'd thought she was in love with Blaine Thomas.

It's not the same.

But wasn't it? She was kidding herself, denying the facts. She wanted to believe he was Keegan Winslow. To think otherwise meant she had to face the fact she was a poor judge of character, that she possessed some fatal flaw that attracted her to dark and dangerous men.

Whimpering, Wren returned the shotgun to the gun cabinet, careful not to step on the sharp shards littering the carpet. In her fear and haste she had broken the glass when she'd been unable to locate the key.

Had her spirits ever been so heavy, her existence so black? Yes. After her parents died, when she'd awakened in the hospital to have the doctors tell her she might never walk again. That had been bad. But this was awful, too. Much worse than what had happened with Blaine Thomas. Blaine had taken her money and her pride, but he had not broken her heart. She let out a high-pitched wail.

Keegan had wished that she might find love. Unfortunately, she had. With him. No matter how much she might wish it wasn't true, she couldn't refuse the feelings that churned inside her whenever she thought of him. He needed her, whether he knew it or not, and she needed him.

Both of them had so much sorrow in their past, it was such a shame they couldn't reach out to each other and express their true feelings. But how could they, when she wasn't even sure of the man's identity? She shook her head. He could not be Connor Heller, no matter how damning the evidence appeared. She would not have such strong feelings for a man who could start a fire with the express purpose of killing a family. Whatever his faults, Wren knew Keegan was incapable of such an act.

But he was consumed with revenge. With good reason, Wren could grant him that, but how could a man learn to love again if his heart was filled with hate?

Despondent, Wren dropped onto the couch. Why had he come into her life, raised her expectations, made her start living again and then cruelly dashed her hopes?

She stared glumly at the lights on the Christmas tree. She'd been right after all to close herself off from people, to pick loneliness over love. She had taken a chance and all she'd gotten for her efforts was a big old pile of pain.

Perhaps, the part of her that declined to give up whispered, *perhaps once he's captured Connor Heller and sent him to prison, Keegan will come back for you.*

Mentally, Wren squelched that romantic notion and hardened her heart. She didn't live in the world of romance novels, she lived a harsh cold reality. She was a crippled spinster with nothing but a run-down dairy farm and a poorly paying teaching job as her future. She might as well get used to the idea that no Prince Charming, hell, not even a damaged bad boy, was going to come rescue her from her fate. This was her life and she had to come to grips with it.

Self-pity, stronger than anything she'd experienced since the accident that took her parents' lives, welled inside her. Wren buried her face in her hands and sobbed.

A few minutes later, a knock at her door had her swiping at her tears. Midnight on Christmas Eve. She no longer believed in Santa. There was only one other person it could be.

Wren sprang from the couch and hurried across the room. "Keegan!" she cried out and threw open the door.

Chapter Ten

But it wasn't Keegan Winslow standing on her porch.

Wren's spirits plummeted at the same moment a spiral of fear coiled inside her stomach. She might have thought Keegan was ominous that night he'd appeared at her door, but this character was straight from a horror movie.

The man was big. Bigger than Keegan, with massive shoulders that filled the doorway. He had long stringy black hair that grew past his shoulders and a scraggly beard that almost obscured his thick neck. His eyes were small and dark, his lips thick and ugly. Pockmarks marred his complexion. His overcoat was stained and dirty and he emitted a rather unpleasant odor.

Wren gasped and took a step back.

He pushed her aside, slamming the door behind him and shifting his beady-eyed gaze around the kitchen.

"W-who are you?" she demanded but Wren knew the answer before he even spoke.

The thug grinned wickedly, revealing a row of

crooked yellowed teeth. "My name's Connor Heller, and I come to pay you a little visit, ma'am."

His politeness was chilling. More so than rank profanity would have been.

Wren drew herself up and tried her best not to show him any fear. "You're not invited."

"Ah." He faked a disappointed expression and shook his shaggy head. "That's too bad."

"I'm going to have to ask you to leave, Mr. Heller."

"What's the matter? I ain't as cute as your boyfriend?"

"If you're not out of here in the next thirty seconds, I'm calling the sheriff."

"You can't, sweet thing. I cut your telephone lines about three days ago and the storm has kept the phone company sorta busy. They haven't had a chance to make it out here."

Wren sucked in her breath. Her phone lines *had* been cut. Not by Keegan, but by this man.

"How do you know that?" she whispered, feeling herself rapidly losing her control.

"I've been watching you." Heller breathed heavily, making Wren think rather inanely, of the actor Peter Lorre. "Waiting for your cop boyfriend to leave."

"I don't know what you're talking about."

"Sure you do. I saw you playing kissy-face with Winslow."

"You were spying on us!"

"Yep."

Wren shuddered. "Why did you cut my phone lines?" she asked.

"Hell, I was gonna invite myself in three days ago. Imagine my surprise when Keegan Winslow beat me to it." Heller snorted. "Some detective he is. Couldn't find his rear end with both hands. I was ten yards away and he had no idea I was here.''

Feeling the color drain from her face, Wren leaned against the wall and tried to think. ''You've been hiding here all along?''

''Yep. Been holed up in your root cellar all this time.''

''Why?''

''Waitin' for a chance to visit my pap for Christmas.''

''So why my house?'' She fisted her hands on her hips, hoping to seem calm, and recoup her bluff.

''You were close. And alone.''

''Keegan was here.''

''Yeah. He ruined all my plans.'' Heller's eyes gleamed as his gaze roved over Wren's body. ''Until now.''

''He's coming back,'' she said.

''No, he's not. He's looking for me.''

''He'll find you.''

''That idiot? Not likely. He's been trailing me for six months without any luck.''

''You sound pretty sure of yourself.''

''Why shouldn't I be?''

''It's all over the radio you've been spotted in Stephenville. There's an all-points bulletin out on you.''

That got his attention. He looked startled. ''I deluded them before, I'll do it again.''

It was on the tip of Wren's tongue to tell him the word was ''eluded,'' but she kept her mouth shut. Let the oaf remain ignorant. It was doubtful he'd even finished high school.

''Hey,'' Heller asked, changing the subject. ''Do you got anything to eat?''

Before she could answer, he went over to the refrigerator and flung open the door. He found a leftover Cornish game hen and began to rip at it with his teeth. He stuffed the food into his face, chewed lewdly, then threw the bones in the trash can and licked his thick fingers. "You're a damned good cook."

Was she supposed to thank him for the compliment? Wren decided proper etiquette wasn't required in this situation.

"Why'd you do it?" Wren asked instead. "Why did you murder Keegan's wife and baby daughter?"

A feral expression crossed Heller's features. "He killed my little brother, Victor. I had to make him pay."

"It didn't solve anything, did it?" she said, lecturing him the way she longed to lecture Keegan. "You went to prison and now you're on the run. Plus, your brother is still dead."

"I got the satisfaction of hurting your boyfriend. Let him have a dose of his own medicine. Cops are so full of themselves. They like dishing it out but when it comes to taking it, they're sissies."

She winced against his cold reply. "What makes you think Keegan is my boyfriend?"

"I saw you together. The way he looked at you. The way you two fought."

Wren remembered the heated exchange between her and Keegan right here in this kitchen when he'd lost control of his temper and lashed out at her.

"He's got the hots for you. Bad." Heller raked another lecherous gaze over her body, making Wren wish she was wearing a suit of armor. "Personally, I don't see it. You're mousy and you don't wear near enough makeup. But I suppose he was pretty hard up."

She ignored his insult.

"Then again, Winslow's wife wasn't much of a

looker either. Guess he prefers the sweet, innocent types,'' Heller mused.

"You think—because we argued—it means Keegan cares about me?'' Wren pushed her bangs from her face, curious to hear what the man had to say.

"Passion, baby. I spied on him and his old lady for three weeks before I torched the house. Guess what? They never fought. Ever. Don't you consider that a little strange?''

Passion? Keegan passionate about her? Could it be true? Wren's heart gave a little bump at the possibility.

"Do you?'' Wren didn't know why she was asking this man's opinion other than she longed to explore her undeniable attraction to Keegan Winslow.

"Hey, if you can't get het up enough over someone to fight with them, how you gonna make sparks under the covers?''

The thought of anyone making sparks with this disgusting man sent a shiver of loathing running through her body. This was ridiculous. Why was she standing here talking to this person? She had no idea of his intentions, but surely they weren't good. She should be planning an escape. Either make a dash for the gun cabinet or try to get out the back door before he could catch her.

"You're a very crude man,'' she said. She was closer to the door than to the gun cabinet but he could easily step out and block her way.

"I admit I ain't no dandy. Not like your Winslow,'' he spoke in a mocking, singsongy voice.

"Stop making fun of Keegan,'' Wren replied hotly. "He's a kind, upstanding man and I hope he puts you back behind bars for the rest of your natural life.''

"You got a crush on him, don't you," Heller crowed. "That's all I wanted to know."

"I do not," Wren denied but she knew the proof was on her face for this creep to read. She did not hide her emotions well. She did love Keegan Winslow, with all her heart and soul, and she was sorry she'd ever doubted him for even one minute.

"Oh, this is great," Heller giggled a high-pitched laugh that sent chills marching down Wren's spine. "I had to be sure."

"Sure of what?" Wren asked, horror squeezing her chest at the look on his face.

He rubbed his palms together and advanced upon her. "I had to be sure he cared about you."

"Why?" Wren's voice was shrill, her back pressed stickily against the wall.

"So I can kill you."

Her knees buckled and she swayed on her feet. The man was insane. There was no other explanation for his sick behavior.

"This way," Heller explained, rubbing his palms together with delight. "I can get revenge on Winslow twice!"

Keegan trudged through the snow, the wind battering his body. He couldn't stop thinking about the look on Wren's face when he'd turned his back on her and walked out the door.

He'd been cruel, he knew that. *Cruel to be kind.* The words from an old song ran through his mind. He'd always thought it was a stupid song, but now he understood. Sometimes it was much kinder to be cruel and break someone's heart than it was to allow them to love you when you had nothing to offer. It was better this way. Keegan had no business in Wren's life and she certainly had no place in his. If he could indeed term his pitiful existence a life.

Jamming his hands deeper into his pockets, Keegan trailed the dark, flat ribbon of road stretching out before him. The ankle-deep snow accentuated his loneliness, heightened his feelings of desolation.

Why did his heart ache clean through to his bones? Why did he feel as if he'd just lost the one thing in his life that had made him human again? In the eighteen months since Maggie and Katie's murders, he'd become a feral animal living to find and punish his enemy, and nothing had deterred him from his goal. Until Wren.

Wren. A miracle. A Christmas gift from heaven. His chance at salvation and he'd blown it.

He couldn't let go of his anger, release himself from his vow of revenge. Because if he relinquished his rage, what would sustain him? Wren's love? How could she love him? He was nothing but a shell of his former self. An embittered ex-cop who wanted nothing more to do with home and family and commitment.

Soon enough, she would realize he wasn't worth loving. That he'd been all used up. Then she'd leave him and he'd be worse off than where he started—in monstrous emotional pain but without the sharp edge of his anger to keep him from falling apart.

"Think about Heller," he told himself. "Focus on catching the man. You're so close. Forget Wren Matthews."

But he could not. Not even when he squeezed his eyes tightly closed. What was he doing stumbling around out here in the darkness? What the hell did he expect to find?

Keegan wrapped his hand around the Magnum, seeking comfort, but for once the sturdy metal failed to lift his spirits. "Concentrate," he told himself.

"You've got a mission to complete. Remember what Heller did to Maggie and Katie. He must pay."

Killing Heller won't bring them back. The words floated starkly through his mind.

No, but it would go a long way in easing his pain. Keegan gritted his teeth and recited the rhetoric that had kept him putting one foot in front of the other for so long.

Really? his superego questioned, taunting him. *Since when did hate ever relieve suffering? Hatred only generates more hate.*

That concept stopped him cold. Keegan stood alone on the desolate country road, wind whipping past his ears, snow bunching beneath his feet. Fence posts loomed out of the shadows like misbegotten soldiers accentuating his isolation, heightening his loneliness.

During the past six months Keegan had been able to turn off his conscience, to ignore any and all niggling doubts about the correctness of his actions, but since he'd encountered Wren, the hardness in his heart had started to dissolve. Until this moment he hadn't realized what the last few days with her had actually meant to him.

The welcoming smiles she lavished on him, the nourishing food she prepared, the tenderness she showed him had served to cleanse a small piece of his sullied soul.

Wren was light and life. When he thought of her his heart filled to bursting. Wren. Sweet, innocent, insecure because of her limp.

It disturbed Keegan that she allowed a small physical imperfection to color her opinion of herself. She had no reason to be insecure. She was a hell of a woman. Strong and brave. Quiet and wise. If only he could make her see that.

He reached up to finger the scarf around his neck. The scarf she'd knitted him. Wren had given him her love and he'd refused her offering, out of fear.

What was he so afraid of? Living? Loving? Getting hurt? Keegan sucked in his breath as his emotions warred.

Love or hate? Revenge or clemency? Darkness or daybreak?

Cold air invaded his lungs and they ached with the effort of expanding. The vein at his temple throbbed. He could not continue to entertain both passions. He either loved or he hated. He was angry or merciful. Vengeful or lenient. In that moment, Keegan knew he had to make a choice.

Wren Matthews or Connor Heller.

Behind him lay salvation, ahead eternal damnation.

Fresh snow drifted from the sky and rested on his collar. Keegan turned his face upward.

"Give me a sign," he spoke softly to the heavens, praying for the first time since the fire had obliterated his life. "Show me what to do."

He waited in the silence, his hands clenched at his sides.

Nothing happened. What had he expected? A lightning bolt?

His nose and ears tingled with cold. His toes felt heavy inside his boots. His pulse pushed against his veins in a restless rhythm.

Would there be an answer? A sign? If not on Christmas morning, then when?

Listen. Listen with your heart. The words flew into his mind.

Keegan cocked his head, strained his ears. The wind whipped and whistled. In the distance he saw the glow of Wren's Christmas lights winking merrily into the night, calling him back to her warm shelter.

And then he heard something.

Faint. Distant. But something.

What? It was too far away to identify. He frowned and concentrated on the sound.

Music.

Keegan swiveled, looked about him. How could there be music? There were no houses, or cars, or people. No radios or televisions or compact-disc players. Nothing but fresh snow, bare trees and empty fields.

Still, he heard it and the music gradually grew louder until he could identify the song.

"Away in a Manger."

Sung by a woman.

His wife's voice, quirkily out of tune.

No!

Keegan clamped his gloved hands over his ears. But the sound grew louder still until it was a roaring hum inside his head.

"What!" he cried out and dropped to his knees, his face peering up at the sky. "What does it mean?"

Then from the drifting snow flurries, he saw something emerge. A gently glowing white light that flickered and expanded until he recognized the slender form of his dead wife, smiling at him.

"Maggie," Keegan whimpered and fell to his knees. He must be hallucinating. Was the fever back? Was he going insane?

He buried his head in his hands and squeezed his eyes shut. The pain searing his heart was almost unbearable.

"She loves you, Keegan."

He opened his eyes but Maggie was still there, the flowing white gown she wore swirling around her in a gauzy haze.

"Who?" he croaked.

"Wren. You could love her too, if you let yourself."

"But...how can I?"

"Let go."

"Let go of what?" He beseeched her.

"Anger, hatred, revenge."

"But what about Heller?"

"It's too late for me and Katie, don't let it be too late for you, Keegan."

Shivers traversed his spine. "Tell me what to do," he begged.

"Love," she replied.

The word reverberated in his brain. The sound resonated like a tuning fork, sending vibrations throughout his body.

Love.

"Wren needs you, and you need her. Don't worry about me and Katie. We're happy now, and safe. We want you to be happy, too."

"I never meant to let you down," Keegan said, tears slipping down his face.

"Keegan, forgive yourself. Go. Love again."

And suddenly a sensation unlike anything he'd ever experienced rushed over him. Peace. Serenity. Tranquility. Every muscle in his body relaxed in response to the gentle heat suffusing his system.

Keegan felt weightless, unfettered, free. The sound of Maggie's voice grew fainter and fainter until it disappeared, leaving his body pulsating with raw energy.

"Maggie?" He rubbed his eyes and stared at the spot where she'd stood but nothing was there. Had Maggie's spirit truly been here or had his imagination concocted the whole thing? Did it matter? The message remained the same.

Love.

Had he been holding on to revenge for Maggie's and Katie's sake, or for his own purposes? Had he been deluding himself all along? Keegan knew the answer. Vengeance was selfish. It destroyed. Only love and forgiveness could make him whole. And he knew where to find that acceptance. All he need do was reach out for the woman he loved.

Wren.

And he did love her, with an intensity that far surpassed anything he'd ever felt for Maggie. He'd loved his wife, yes. But it had been a soft and gentle sort of love, not this all-consuming passion that engulfed him whenever he thought about Wren. His body had never ached for Maggie the way it ached for Wren. Never thirsted the way he was thirsting now for the forgiveness only intimate sharing could bring. Never needed love the way he needed it now.

He got to his feet and withdrew the Magnum from its holster. The gun was a symbol of his hatred. Swallowing hard, he grabbed the pistol by the barrel and flung it far.

Feeling as if a gigantic burden had been lifted from his shoulders Keegan turned and trotted across the field.

"Jingle Bell Rock" played from the transistor radio hunkered on the windowsill.

Wren sat rooted to a chair in the middle of the kitchen floor, her eyes fixed on the drunken man dancing around the room with her Santa Claus apron tied around his head. He looked chillingly demented.

In one hand Connor Heller carried a jar of gasoline,

in the other a whiskey bottle. He had a lit cigarette pinched between his thick lips. His eyes glistened with a bright, evil sheen. He'd scarfed down three loaves of cranberry-walnut bread and the crumbs clung to his dirty beard.

"Ain't this fun?" he slurred, sloshing whiskey on his shirt, as he leaned in close. The apron tails bobbed gaily about his thick shoulders.

Beneath his shirt, she could see the delineation of a handgun tucked in his waistband. Dread rose in her throat, hot and caustic, but she didn't dare let this animal know exactly how much he frightened her.

She said nothing.

He pushed his face next to hers. "I asked you a question."

"Yeah," Wren snapped, "this is a regular laugh a minute."

He threw back his head and let loose with a guffaw. "Boy howdy, you are more fun than Winslow's first woman. She just wanted to scream and cry."

Suddenly, Wren understood Keegan's need for revenge. This filthy animal deserved to be imprisoned for the rest of his natural life. Anger overrode her common sense. She sucked in her breath and told Heller exactly what was on her mind.

"You should be locked up forever."

"No prison can hold me," Heller bragged. "I'll just escape again. That is, if they ever catch me."

"You're scum!"

Wren was a little surprised at her own vehemence but her rage knew no bounds. For the first time in her life she had found someone she truly cared about, but Keegan had been so damaged by what this creep had done to his family that he could not return her devotion. She

nderstood it but it grieved her nonetheless. If Keegan
urt, then she hurt. At this point, it didn't even matter
f Heller burned down the house with her in it. What
vas life without the man she loved?

And love him she did, with a consuming passion. It
idn't matter that they'd known each other only a few
ays. She knew all she needed to know about him. They
vere kindred spirits, linked by pain and suffering. Two
eople who were battered and bruised, but could heal
ach other if they but tried.

*You'll never get the chance to find out. Connor Hel-
r's going to kill you.*

Wren looked into that maniacal face and knew the
uth. She was about to die. Alone. Frightened. And
vithout ever telling Keegan how much she loved him.

Heller's giggling accelerated as he took another slug
f whiskey.

Oh dear God, the man was insane!

Her gaze scanned the kitchen, searching for a weapon.
 large cast iron skillet hung on the rack above the
:ove. It was ten feet away. Could she make it to the
ove before he drew his gun and shot her?

"You know," she said, remaining outwardly calm
rhile internally her mind raced off in a million splin-
red directions. "It is Christmas morning."

"Yeah?" He shook his head and her apron side to
ne side.

"If you kill me on Christmas then I doubt you'll get
ything but coal in your stocking."

He paused, looking at her as if she were nuts and then
ughed nervously. "You trying to tell me that you be-
ve in Santa Claus?"

"No," she said. "I believe in miracles."

"That's good, cause it's gonna take a miracle to save your hide tonight, crip."

Crip. His word echoed Blaine Thomas's long-ago accusation. *Who could love a cripple?*

She'd show this low-life who was crippled!

Ire commingled with determination. She wasn't about to sit like a helpless victim being harangued by this bully while the man she loved trudged alone out there in the ice-encrusted darkness. Whatever it took, she would fight for her life and then she would fight to secure Keegan's love. Wren gritted her teeth, heaved herself from the chair and lunged for the stove.

Her unexpected action threw Heller off guard. He reached to grab her only to discover his hands were full. Surprise flitted across his face but Wren, on the move, barely noticed.

Heller growled.

Wren didn't glance behind her. She couldn't afford to see how close he stood. Instead, she reached forward and grasped the lip of the iron skillet with her fingers.

She felt him grab her flannel nightgown in his fist. He jerked her backward just as she got a firm grip on the skillet's handle. Like a tennis player executing the perfect backhand, Wren rounded on the convict and slammed him a stunning blow on the side of his head.

Heller grunted and dropped to his knees.

Wren wasted no time on triumph. She spun on her heels, hurried for the door and struggled to wrench it open. The thing wouldn't budge.

He locked it. Undo the lock, Wren.

Her breathing came in hard, erratic spurts. Her fingers fumbled with the clasp. She heard Heller stagger to his feet and her pulse leapt in her throat, sending a heated rush of blood through her body and spurring her onward

Go, go, go.

In her headlong haste, she barely perceived the loud clattering noise. A gun? The iron skillet? She cringed. What was Heller doing?

Something splashed behind her. She smelled gasoline. No!

A dry flicking sound. Like a lighter reluctant to spark. Fear crowded her throat.

Whoosh!

She looked over her shoulder. Her kitchen floor danced with flames and a trail of fire was running straight for her. Connor Heller stood behind the blaze, grinning wickedly, blood streaking down the side of his face. Wren got the door open at last and flung herself outside into the frigid night, slipping on the stairs as she did. Knocked off her feet, she grasped the railing at the same time her mouth dropped open in horror.

Heller's shriek of maniacal laughter reverberated throughout the night. Wren regained her balance and limped across the yard.

"Burn, baby, burn!" Heller shouted.

Wren realized she should run, but she stood and stared in horror. Her house was on fire.

Chapter Eleven

A frantic urgency built in Keegan's chest. Wren needed him. Desperately. How he knew this he would be hard pressed to say, but he knew something was wrong. It was as if they were joined by some bizarre psychic link and after what had happened to him out there in the field when he'd spoken to God and received an answer from Maggie, Keegan wasn't about to take his premonition lightly.

But Wren's house lay a half a mile in the distance and already his breathing was labored. Damn this weakness. Keegan gritted his teeth and pushed himself onward.

Wren.

He could think of nothing but her. From her kind, encouraging smile to her sweet lavender scent. He recalled the way her skin had felt brushing against his when she'd shaved his face. He remembered the melodious sounds of her tinkling laughter. He could not for get the lengths she'd gone to in order to make this a special Christmas for him.

And he'd thrown it back in her face.

All thoughts of revenge had disappeared. To hell with Connor Heller. Wren needed him and he wasn't about to let her down the way he'd disappointed Maggie. God had given him a second chance and he was grabbing at it with both hands.

If nothing else, Heller had taught him that. It had been an awful way to learn a hard lesson, but Keegan would never again take a woman's love for granted.

He trudged across the field, head down, coat collar up against the wind. When he got back to the farmhouse, he was going to take Wren into his arms, kiss her gently and apologize for his behavior.

The Christmas lights winked brighter as he drew closer. Keegan lifted his face. Fear rippled over him, fear that was even more compelling than on that awful night eighteen months earlier.

He smelled the smoke before he saw the flames.

"No!" he screamed the words popping from him in horrible déjà vu. He was caught in some hideous nightmare. There simply could not be another fire. He could not, would not, lose someone else he loved.

Heller.

There could be no other explanation.

Ignoring the pain in his lungs, the aching in his legs, Keegan ran, his knees pumping high, his heart pounding with terror.

The footprints he'd discovered in the snow yesterday morning *had* belonged to Heller. Deep in his gut he'd known it, yet denied it. It seemed too coincidental but it had to be true. While he'd been hunting Heller, the murderer had been tracking him!

"Wren!" Keegan shouted and prayed that this time, he would not be too late.

Wren peeked over at the house. The flames were dying down, having already consumed the gasoline. Perhaps her family homestead would not be lost in a fire after all.

But what about Heller? Where had he gone?

Fear returned with a vengeance.

As if on cue, Heller came around the side of the house, emitting a loud war whoop. Before she could scramble away, he was there, grabbing her hair and pulling her to her feet.

Wren kicked at him.

Heller dodged and laughed grimly.

Wren cursed, using words she'd never before uttered in her life.

Heller clamped his arm around her neck and squeezed. He pulled the gun from his waistband and aimed it at her. "Ready or not, it's time to meet your maker."

Wren closed her eyes and prayed. She thought of Keegan and how she would never see him again. Never feel those strong arms holding her tightly, never again taste the honey of his lips, never savor the special experience of making love to him.

"Let her go, Heller." Keegan's voice exploded into the fray like a live hand grenade blowing into a foxhole. "She's got nothing to do with this. Your beef's with me."

Relief flooded Wren. Tremors of joy raced through her body. Keegan! He'd come back for her! Blinking, she squirmed in Heller's arm, trying hard to get a better view of her beloved.

Keegan stood like a gunslinger, tall and imposing, hi

ands resting on his hips, a scowl marring his handsome
eatures. "You heard me, Heller, release her."

"Whatcha gonna do, Mr. Policeman, spit on me?"

That's when Wren noticed Keegan was unarmed.
Where was the Magnum? Her stomach plunged to her
eet. They were going to die. Both of them.

"Watch out, Keegan. He's got a gun!" she cried.

Heller turned and pointed the gun at Keegan. "I'm
gonna finish what I started eighteen months ago, Win-
low. Prepare to die."

No! Wren's brain screamed. Not while she had an
unce of breath left in her. In one quick second, she
bbed Heller hard in the rib cage with her elbow and
od heavily on his instep.

Heller yelped. The pistol jumped in his hand, spat
arks into the air, the noise deafening.

Wren's teeth came down on her bottom lip. Her ears
ng. Her eyes watered. She smelled gunpowder and
sted her own blood.

What happened next passed in a blinding blur. Connor
eller stumbled backward. Keegan lunged forward,
ocking the murderer to the ground.

The impact dislodged the gun from Heller's grip. It
w into the air. Keegan caught the pistol and straddled
e man's prostrate body. Gripping the barrel with both
nds he pressed the nose against Heller's chin.

"Just give me an excuse," Keegan wheezed.

"This is your chance, Winslow. Go ahead, kill me!"
eller glared up at him.

"Don't do it," Wren urged. "Don't give him the sat-
faction." She watched the emotions play over Kee-
n's face—anger, hatred, rancor. She saw his jaw
nch, his lips tighten.

"Do it," Heller goaded. "I can't go back to prison."

"If you kill him then you're no different than him
Don't give in to revenge, Keegan. Please." Wren laced
her hands together. "Don't perpetuate the violence."

Keegan cocked the trigger.

He's going to kill him, she thought and turned her
head. She braced herself for the shots that never came.

"Get up," Keegan said hoarsely. "Now." He
marched Heller into the back of Wren's pickup and hog
tied him with a rope Wren brought from the barn.

"I'll freeze to death," Heller whined.

"If you're lucky." Giving him a hard stare, Keegan
grabbed a saddle blanket from the corner and threw it
over the man.

Wren waited, gently rubbing her injured lip.

"Are you all right?" he asked.

"I think so. I got out of the house before I wa
burned."

"Let me examine you."

His gut torqued to think she could have been seared
the way he had been burned. Tenderly he lifted her hair
surveyed her back and neck. Relief flooded his body
when he saw there was no damage to her precious skin
"You're a little red around your neck and your pretty
hair is singed but nothing serious."

"Oh, Keegan."

"It's okay. I'm here." He kissed her temple, pressed
her head against his chest.

She sank against him and he held her for the moment
savoring the feel of her. Then at last cold forced him to
pry himself away. He handed her Heller's gun. "Keep
this trained on him while I go make sure the fire's out
then we're going to the police."

Keegan was nervous about leaving her alone with
Heller, but the man was tied securely and Wren ha

shown remarkable bravery just now. His chest swelled with pride. She was one hell of a woman.

Walking into the house, he was pleased to discover the fire damage was minimal. The newspapers in the entryway still smoldered so he poured water on them. Smoke's acrid reek wafted up to him, reminding Keegan this story could have had a much different ending.

He sagged against the refrigerator as spent adrenaline circulated through his system, causing him to feel jittery and sharp-edged. He didn't even want to imagine what he would have found had he been only one minute later.

Shaking off the sensation, he made sure the fire was completely extinguished before locking the door, retrieving Wren's coat and heading over to join her at the pickup.

He helped her inside. She smiled at him and that simple action warmed him straight to his soul. Although it was only a few miles into Stephenville, the ice and snow hampered their progress. Focusing his gaze on the road, Keegan concentrated on the drive, his mind whirling with the things he wanted to say to the woman beside him.

Even before Maggie's death he'd never been one to express himself freely and now that he was here with Wren, he didn't quite know how to go about revealing what was in his heart. Suddenly, he was terrified that she did not feel the things for him that he felt for her.

They arrived at the police station a half hour later. It was another two hours after that before they'd completed the paperwork involved with the arrest and been okayed by the sheriff to leave. The drive home was silent. Keegan's anxiety grew. What was Wren thinking? Was she wishing she'd never set eyes on him? Was she filled with regret?

He wasn't sorry that he'd decided against killing Heller. He was glad he'd been able to relinquish his revenge at the final moment. Yet he remained uncertain about his destiny. Where did he go from here? Did the future include Wren?

Keegan pulled into the driveway and cut the engine, just as the sun peeped over the horizon, illuminating the snow stretched across the ground in a silvery winter wonderland.

"Some Christmas morning, huh?"

"I'm so proud of you," Wren said, the tightness in her voice throwing him off guard.

Back there on the road when he'd had his epiphany, everything had seemed so clear, so certain. But at this moment, looking at Wren, Keegan wasn't so sure. Did she want him?

Her cheeks were red, her brown hair a wild tumble about her shoulders. Soot stained her neck. Her bottom lip was swollen but she was the most beautiful thing he'd ever seen. He felt tongue-tied and awkward in her presence.

"You're proud of me?" he asked.

"Yes."

"You're the unbelievable one. Damn, darling, you were so brave. If you hadn't elbowed Heller when you did, we'd both be dead." He reached across the seat to cup her chin in his palm.

A tear trickled down her cheek but she swiped it away with the back of her hand.

"What's wrong?" he asked, alarmed.

"Nothing."

"But you're crying." The sight tugged at his chest with an intensity that caused physical pain.

"Tears of joy."

"You're happy?" He frowned, confused.

"You didn't kill Heller."

"No."

"Why not? You had every right. He murdered your family, destroyed your life."

"I couldn't."

"Why not?"

"Because of you."

"Me?" She looked into his eyes and Keegan felt the last chunk of ice inside him melt. He couldn't hold back any secrets. Not from her.

"You taught me about kindness, Wren Matthews. You reminded me what it was like to be human. I'd forgotten. I was so caught up in getting even with Heller that I couldn't see revenge had turned me into a cold, unforgiving man. Maggie wouldn't have wanted that for me."

Wren nodded. He still loved his wife. How could he not? She'd been tragically murdered. He could never forget her. Wren pulled away from him and glanced down at her hands. How could she hope to compete with a dead woman?

"You've taught me a lot, too," she said, pushing aside the ache.

"I have?"

"When I met you I realized there was someone with more sorrows than me. You made me forget my own problems while helping you solve yours and in the course of that lesson I came back to myself again. The way I was before my parents died, before injury, before Blaine Thomas took advantage of me and shattered my confidence. You gave me back my joy, Keegan Winslow, and I'll never forget you for that."

"I'll never forget you either." His gut torqued. She

was dismissing him. She hadn't invited him to stay and he didn't know how to ask.

"I guess you'll be leaving soon," she said, her tone wistful.

"Does that mean you've already filled the dairy hand position?" Keegan could hardly contain his grin. She didn't sound as if she wanted him to leave.

"The position is still available." She raised her head and met his stare. "Are you applying?"

"I'm not sure if I'm qualified."

"You know your way around a milking machine. And you're a dab hand with a welding torch."

This time he let the grin spread all the way across his face. "I'd be honored if you'd let me stay."

"Then the job is yours."

"Are we talking about more than employment?" he asked. "I need to know."

"Haven't you guessed how I feel?"

He nodded. "Yeah. But I'm scared. I've still got a long way to go, Wren, before I'm back in the land of the living. There's a lot of old baggage that needs cleaning up. I loved my wife and daughter, yes, but that doesn't mean I can't learn to love again. You've gotten under my skin, Wren Matthews, though heaven knows I have done my damnedest to push you away."

"Keegan…I…please, don't toy with my heart. I can't be your tutor, your teacher. I have needs, too."

"Oh, sweetheart, I know that." He reached across the seat and drew her into his arms. He buried his nose in her hair and inhaled, identifying her special scent masked beneath the soot and smoke. "I want to meet all your needs, fulfill all your expectations, but at the same time I want to allow you to be your own woman. I made that mistake in my marriage. I always had to be the strong protector. It was hard for me to accept help. I don't want to make those same mistakes with you.''

Trembling with emotion, Wren turned her face up to him and let his mouth tenderly taste her bruised lips. His touch was so gentle, she breathed in a sigh and floated on it, drifting away on their closeness.

All her life she'd dreamt of being held this way, of being cared for and treated with kindness. Keegan's concern for her was real, not like Blaine. Even though he wasn't yet ready for a deeper commitment, she knew time healed all wounds. Just as her own had healed, Keegan's would, too.

She was tired of living in the darkness, of being alone and praying for someone special. She was tired of being afraid, of mistrusting men. Neither of them was a stranger to pain. He had loved once, he could do it again. He was here now and she could wait for him.

Returning his kiss, she squeezed him tightly. "I love you, Keegan Winslow, with all my heart and soul."

"Wren, Wren," he groaned. "Help me learn to start loving again."

"Yes, Keegan," she said. "Yes."

In that moment, she knew that eventually they would both be ready for so much more. The future shone brighter than it ever had before. Her instincts told her they would make it. She looked at the rising sun, shining fresh and new against the snow.

"Merry Christmas, Keegan," she whispered. And with that heartfelt sentiment, she drew him into her arms and held him close for a very long time.

Epilogue

The urge to love had grown, nurtured to a roaring blaze by Wren's quiet attention. Keegan stood on the front lawn, his gaze scanning the area. It was Christmas Eve again, but this time the weather was a far cry from a year ago. Just as he himself was far different from that brooding vengeful man he'd been. The sun shone brightly, and the temperature was a balmy sixty-two degrees.

The yard was decorated with a life-size plastic Santa and nine reindeer pulling a sleigh. Elves peeped from behind trees and around the corners. Over a thousand light strands ran along the house and the fence railing, blinking in colorful harmony.

Keegan looked at his and Wren's handiwork and grinned. The guests would be arriving soon and he couldn't wait to see the expression on their faces when they got a load of the Christmas scene.

A warm, fizzy sensation enveloped him as he turned to head up the sidewalk. He hadn't for one instant regretted the decision he'd made a year ago when he'd moved into the loft over the barn.

The bucolic environment had a soothing effect on him, reminding him of his past and putting him in touch with his roots. He'd discovered he loved working the dairy more than he'd ever enjoyed police work, and under his care the farm had thrived. Already the herd had grown from seventeen to twenty-five head and they hoped to add more in the next few months.

He and Wren had courted slowly, dating like any other couple, going to the movies, taking long walks through the woods, sitting quietly by the fire after supper. He picked Wren wild flowers in the spring and had taken her on picnics. In the summer they sat outside and gazed at the stars. They often stayed up late, talking far into the night.

Every day he awoke with the knowledge that the past was behind him and that he was loved. Each day with Wren grew better and better as he began to appreciate the simple things in life. The sound of her laughter, the touch of her fingers on his arms, the shining expression in her eyes when she looked at him.

The physical attraction between them built stronger and harder until one day in late September, when Keegan didn't think he could last a single second longer without making love to Wren, he asked her to marry him. They'd exchanged their vows right here in the farmhouse with Reverend Duvall performing the ceremony.

Because of the dairy they couldn't stay away long, so the honeymoon had been a weekend trip to San Antonio. It had been the sexiest, most romantic weekend of his life. Even now, simply thinking about Wren's receptiveness caused a high flush to rise to his cheeks.

He wiped his boots on the welcome mat and then stepped inside the back door. His heart swelled, brimming with joyous emotion as the smells of Christmas teased his nostrils. Peppermint, cinnamon, pumpkin. Roast turkey, home-baked bread and apple cider.

A large pot of poinsettias rested on the kitchen table. If he craned his neck, Keegan could see the Christmas tree overflowing with presents. This year, he'd bought Wren a dozen gifts. Sprigs of mistletoe hung from the doorway and even though it wasn't cold outside, there was a small fire in the fireplace.

"Honey?" he called. "Where are you?"

Wren stepped from the bedroom, closing the door behind her. She moved down the hall.

Keegan's heart caught in his throat at the sight of her. She was so beautiful. Wren wore a red velvet dress with black patent leather pumps and the string of pearls he'd gotten her for her thirtieth birthday. She smiled at him but he saw there were tears shining in her brown eyes.

"Wren? What's wrong?"

"I just got off the phone," she said. "With Dr. Winston."

His stomach lurched. Not bad news! "Are you sick?" Keegan asked, rushing to her side and taking her elbow. He couldn't bear it if something were to happen to her.

"No," she said, "not sick."

Keegan stared. "Then why would Dr. Winston call you on Christmas Eve..." He trailed off as realization dawned. "You're pregnant?" Elation thrilled through him. They were going to have a baby.

Wren nodded, her smile widening. "Is that okay? Are you happy? I mean, we never talked about it."

Sweeping her into his arms, Keegan twirled her off her feet. "I'm ecstatic."

"I've been thinking," Wren said, after he'd dropped a round of kisses on her eyes, her lips, her cheek and chin.

"Yes."

"If it's a girl I'd like to call her Katherine Margaret if that's okay with you."

Wren wanted to name their baby after the family he'd lost? Love for his new bride spread through his whole system, hot, swift and passionate. She was so kind, so giving. He thanked God for her daily.

"That'd be wonderful," he said gruffly.

"And of course if it's a boy he'll be Keegan Junior."

"Have I ever told you I love you?" Keegan asked, cupping her chin in his palm.

"Maybe a time or two." Her eyes twinkled merrily.

"Mrs. Winslow," he growled low in his throat, "I'm afraid I'm going to have to take you into the bedroom and make love to you."

"But the guests are due in an hour and I haven't mashed the potatoes yet!"

"So let them eat lumps." He nibbled on her ear.

Wren sighed her pleasure, relieved and happy that Keegan had taken the news of the baby so well. For the longest time she'd been afraid he wouldn't want children after what had happened to his daughter. So afraid she'd never broached the subject. And even though he'd grown and changed a lot over the last twelve months, she'd still worried that something dark and sad inhibited his heart. It cheered her to know he was ready to try parenthood again. The dream she'd held on to for so many years had finally come true.

"I love you, Keegan Winslow," she declared, wrapping her arms around him.

"And I love you, Wren Matthews Winslow," he said.

"Merry Christmas, Daddy."

Wren snuggled into the curve of Keegan's arm and knew right then and there that the wounds she once thought ran so deep in both of them had been completely healed by love.

*   *   *   *   *

Looking For More Romance?

Visit Romance.net

Check in daily for these and other exciting features:

Hot off the press

View all current titles, and purchase them on-line.

What do the stars have in store for you?

Horoscope

Hot deals

Exclusive offers available only at Romance.net

Plus, don't miss our interactive quizzes, contests and bonus gifts.

PWEB

COMING NEXT MONTH

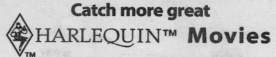

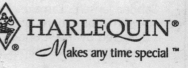